SHATTERED

THE CURSE TRILOGY BOOK 3

NICOLE MARSH
CASSY JAMES

Copyright © 2020 by Nicole Marsh & Cassy James. All rights reserved.

Cover Art by Spellbinding Designs

No part of this book may be reproduced in any form or by any electronic or mechanical means, including information storage and retrieval systems, without written permission from the author, except for the use of brief quotations in a book review. This is a work of fiction. Names, characters, businesses, places, events, and incidents are either the product of the author's imagination or used simply for the purpose of furthering the storyline and do not represent the institutions or places of business in any way. Any resemblance to actual persons, living or dead, or actual events is purely coincidental or used for fictional purposes.

This book is the continuation of a series and cannot be read as a standalone. It does contain some material that may be triggering to some readers.

If you have not read the first book in the series:
Cursed: The Curse Trilogy Book 1
It can be found at: www.books2read.com/TCT1

If you have not read the second book in the series:
Bound: The Curse Trilogy Book 2
It can be found at: www.books2read.com/TCT2

MIRABELLA LOVE

On my eighteenth birthday, my entire life changed with a simple truth.

Magic is real.

I thought earning my witches license would be the hardest challenge I would face, but that was merely the tip of the iceberg. Suddenly, an entire race of magical creatures is counting on me. And the people I thought I could trust... may not be trustworthy.

With a group of unexpected companions, I flee the only home I've ever known in search of answers. Together we unveil an entire slew of secrets that have been woven together over centuries, but even that may not be enough.

Will we be able to find the cure before it's too late?

CONTENTS

1.	The Incident	1
2.	The Magic	12
3.	The Disappointment	21
4.	The Archives	31
5.	The Deception	42
6.	The Departure	53
7.	The Lair	62
8.	The Suggestion	75
9.	The Ally	87
10.	The Sieves	101
11.	The Reveal	113
12.	The Tryst	120
13.	The Premonition	133
14.	The Plan	145
15.	The Return	156
16.	The Rat	168
17.	The Spring	177
18.	The Potion	187
19.	The Cure	197
20.	The Throwdown	205
21.	The Idea	216
	Epilogue	227
	Interested in news about books by Nicole Marsh?	239
	Interested in news about books by Cassy James?	241
	Books by Nicole Marsh	243
	Books by Cassy James	245
	Reviews	247

1

THE INCIDENT

Mirabella

"I'll escort you to your quarters," Archibald Golden states, after we've established the reason for our small crews' arrival.

"Err... that's okay. I'm sure someone, literally anyone else, could escort us. You probably have more important things to do than show us to our accommodations," I protest, not wanting to spend any more time in Coven Leader Golden's presence. The last few hours of questioning in a giant conference room were more than enough already.

"No, no, I insist," Mr. Golden states, waving his hand in the air as if he's brushing my worries aside like a pesky fly.

"Really, we're fine," I protest again, feebly.

"Ahh, I just need to think of a building that has five

empty rooms," he mutters, pivoting on his heel and stepping a few feet away while he thinks.

"We could double up in rooms, it's no trouble. We just appreciate the ability to use your archives and your willingness to host us with such limited notice," Marc interjects, shooting a beaming smile at Mr. Golden.

I look at Marc, trying to convey gratitude with my eyes. He shoots me a quizzical look, so I'm not quite sure that the expression sent the appropriate message.

"Absolutely not," Mr. Golden responds adamantly. "My coven would never cram visitors into one room, we have plenty of space, especially for such esteemed guests. In fact, I have just the place, although it is a bit of a trek. It will give you the chance to see the city, however."

"Sounds great," Marc replies, halfheartedly. A beaming smile still sits across his lips; however, the expression doesn't quite reach his eyes.

My gaze scans Vlad, Alex, and Sylvia. It's obvious that everyone is barely holding it together. Following the stress of our rapid escape from Florence through the portal, then the hours of questioning we endured following our arrival, it isn't too surprising, but I wish there was a way to hurry Mr. Golden.

He finally moves to the door, holding it open and beckoning for us to follow. I want to groan in relief at the thought of collapsing into a bed, but thankfully I'm able to contain the sound, barely.

Mr. Golden leads us out of the pink crystal building in a winding path and eventually we emerge onto the cobbled streets of Haven. The road seems like it's for pedestrian use only, as hover discs fill the air space above, transporting witches between buildings and out of the city.

Tearing my gaze away from the sky, I glance at the shops lining the cobbled road. Once we were accepted into the town by the coven, a spell seemed to lift. All the words on the signs that appeared to be gibberish are suddenly legible.

Mr. Golden marches us past the "Ingredient Shop", "Witches Brewery", and "Witch Cream" shops. I stare intently into each window, wondering if we'll have an opportunity to come back this way soon.

I'm torn from my thoughts when I suddenly slam into a solid wall of rock-hard muscle. Bouncing off upon impact, I immediately hit the hard cobblestone for the second time today and emit an "oomph".

Looking up, I spot Alex, who came to a dead stop in the middle of the road for no reason. He twirls around, his expression turning panicked until he spots me sprawled rather ungracefully across the hard ground. "Oh, shit Mira, sorry." He offers his hand to help me up, but no other explanation.

I place my palm into his, using the grip to assist me to my feet. Instead of releasing me, Alex intertwines our fingers and slows his pace so we're able to walk side by side. He leads me a few feet away to join the rest of the group clustering at the entrance of a tall, pink building nearby.

Forgetting our hands are connected, I pause at the edge of our crew. My gaze floats over the cylindrical bottom of the tower, drifting upwards until I'm forced to crane my neck. The building stretches for what seems like miles, ending in the sky at a thin, pointed top.

I scan the surrounding area and spot the large, pink castle-like structure just to the left of the building. To the right is an empty expanse. Some distance away sits another building comprised of the crystalline material, only this one starts with a square base, graduating into a thin rectangle as it reaches for the clouds.

My mystified eyes finally connect with Mr. Golden's and he nods his head once, as if he was waiting to regain my attention. "This is Guest Building H," he announces, opening his arms wide to encompass the building in front of us. "You will live here for the duration of your stay in Haven."

"It's a very nice building, sir. Everything in Haven is spectacular," Sylvia chimes in with a sickly, sweet smile.

Mr. Golden returns the look with one more genuine, apparently unable to discern Sylvia's face lacks any genuine happiness. "I'm so glad you're already enjoying your time here. Come, come. I'll show the highlights of the building, then lead you to your rooms to retire. I'm sure you are all very exhausted from your journey."

Maybe he's not as oblivious as I originally thought.

The five of us trail into the building behind Mr. Golden like a gaggle of ducklings. We stop shortly after passing through a double set of doors made of a cloudy, crystal substance. "This is the Lobby," Mr. Golden states and I stifle a groan. If this is what he calls a 'highlight' it's going to take eight years for us to reach our rooms.

Thankfully, his next statement is more interesting and provides hope that a bed may be in my near future. "In every building there's a sign just to the right of the entry. It provides a list of amenities in the building accompanied by the floor for each one." He points to a glimmering sign near the door, and I skim the list.

Our building appears to have typical hotel amenities, to include a restaurant, and both a pool and a sauna. There are a bunch of other rooms listed as well, but I drag my eyes from the sign, wanting to move on.

There will be time to investigate this building, and the others, at a later date.

Mr. Golden claps his hands together once and continues walking. He weaves an odd back and forth path across the room, leading the five of us in a zigzag, only to end up in a straight line from the entry doors.

He stops next to a strange looking cylindrical tube that appears to be made entirely of glass. It reminds me of something you'd see in a gerbil cage, rising out of the floor and continuing into the ceiling with three-quarters made of glass and an opening facing us. Staring at the cylinder I grow concerned. Do we have to crawl up this thing?

Mr. Golden proudly announces, "This is our travel tunnel!"

His words cause my dread to grow tenfold and I ask, "Travel tunnel?"

He nods, grinning from ear to ear. "Yes, of course. One jumps into the tunnel and will be carried to the destination they think of within this building, or any of the buildings in Haven that have the tunnel system. It's simple, efficient, and safe. Would you like to go first?"

"Uhh," I hedge, waiting for one of my friends to interject and save me. I glance around, but they all studiously avoid my gaze and my brain is blanking on excuses. I'm worried a simple 'no, thank you' may be interpreted as ungrateful.

"Do you have an elevator?" I finally ask instead.

Mr. Golden laughs a deep-belly laugh, bending in half and slapping his right palm against his left knee. After a few lingering chuckles escape, he straightens and shakes his head. "You Americans and your sense of humor. We don't get enough of that around here. The tunnels are a thousand times better than elevators. Give it a go, eh? Jump in, you'll see."

With a bracing breath, I finally release my white-knuckled grip on Alex's hand. I take a hesitant step forward, slowly nearing the travel tunnel. "Just jump in?" I squeak, my veins filled with ice cold dread making it hard to form thoughts.

He nods, "Yes. Your room is on the tenth floor, so clear your mind and think 'tenth floor' as you jump inside. The travel tunnel will take care of the rest."

I twist my head, seeking the comfort of a certain amber gaze. My eyes lock with Vlad's and he offers a succinct nod in his own unique brand of encouragement.

Turning back to face Mr. Golden, I inhale deeply, then edge closer to the tunnel. I feel a light breeze emanating outwards and realize there appears to be some sort of cyclone inside. It must be part of the magic that carries users to and from their desired locations.

With one last deep inhale, trying not to overthink it, I hop into the tunnel with both feet. I clear my mind and urge the thought *tenth floor, tenth floor, don't let me get lost* to the front of my brain.

Next thing I know, I'm flung from the tunnel. I brace myself, expecting to hit the floor. Instead, I find myself falling with air whizzing past my head. Flailing my limbs, I attempt to swim in the air, hoping to slow my momentum, confident I will splat against the ground at any second.

How did this go so terribly wrong?

I release a shriek, eyes screwed tightly shut as I prepare for the end. My breath whooshes out of my body upon impact, but instead of becoming a Mira splat on the ground, I find myself nestled inside a... giant net?

Glancing upwards, I see a tunnel posted against a wall in midair, a few stories above me, explaining my fall. As my gaze drifts to the left, I spot a dozen or so of the blue hover discs zooming about.

I attempt to stand, even though adrenaline has turned my legs to wobbly jell-o. The net combined with my poor balance quickly topple me over and I wind up sprawled on my back across the same spot as before.

Another hover disc catches my attention. I trace its movement with my eyes while my thoughts wander, attempting to form a solution to get out of this stupid net. As I watch, the rider takes a turn too quickly and flips the disc over. The rider falls, hitting the net a couple dozen feet to my right.

I realize he's noticeably young, ten at the oldest. Maybe this is the training area for adolescent witches to learn the hover discs. I continue to observe the kid, watching as he clambers up the net using his hands and feet to grip the edges like rungs of a ladder, until he reaches a platform I had previously overlooked.

Exhaling a sigh of relief, I mimic his movements, rolling onto the platform within moments. Remaining on my hands and knees, I gratefully kiss the solid ground, vowing to never repeat that experience again.

Once I stand on my feet, I test my legs with a few

steps. Balance restored, I allow my gaze to swivel around the room, looking for another exit. Unfortunately, the only other way out seems to be a travel tunnel attached to the platform.

Fighting the urge to cry, I approach the tunnel tentatively. This time I will get it right. It can't be that hard if everyone in Haven can do it. My words barely reassure me, but I inhale deeply and jump in anyway. Repeating the process from before, I think *tenth floor, tenth floor, please don't let me end up anywhere embarrassing.*

I'm spit from the tunnel, once again bracing for my impact with the floor. But once again I'm flying through the air at a rapid speed. Opening my mouth to scream at the exact wrong moment, I splash into a pool of water. Instead of inhaling air, I suck in a lungful of water.

Panicking, I shove myself upward with flailing limbs, breaking through the surface with a choking gasp. I continue coughing and spitting, clearing my lungs of the unwelcomed liquid and wondering how the heck I ended up here.

When I finally regain my breath, I open my watery eyes fully and immediately spot a dozen witches in swimsuits doing... water aerobics? At least they were. Now all twenty-four eyes are focused on my fully clothed form, drowning in the center of a large, four-foot-deep pool.

Groaning in mortification, I wave my hands in the air. "I'm okay, I'm so sorry I interrupted," I call out.

Most of the witches face the instructor standing near the far edge of the pool. Only a few eyes remain on me and I wade to the edge of the pool to determine my next move. Before I make it three steps, a breathless Marc appears near the edge of the water.

His gaze scans the room, then the pool. The second he spots my fully clothed form chilling in the water, he turns his head yelling, "Guys, she's in here."

I shift my gaze to the floor, wishing a travel tunnel could suck me right out of the pool and away from this embarrassing situation, but of course that doesn't happen. The tunnels hate me.

The rest of my friends stampede into the room and my cheeks flush further. Why does everyone always have to see me at my worst? Where are all these people on my good hair days?

Resigned, I trudge to the edge of the pool. Vlad offers me a hand, and I use the leverage to exit the water as gracefully as possible and murmur a quiet, "Thank you."

Sylvia dashes over, draping a towel over my shoulders, absorbing a tiny amount of the water dripping from my soaking wet form. "Thanks girl," I whisper and she simply smiles in return.

Vlad adjusts the towel, pulling it tighter around my body before tugging me into his side, soggy clothes and all. He squeezes me, then twists his head to face

Mr. Golden. "Is there any way to get to our rooms besides the travel tunnels?"

Mr. Golden scratches his neck as he replies regretfully, "Ahh, it's the only way to travel between the floors within each building. They've proven to be the safest method, much less dangerous than stairs and elevators." He pauses for a moment, clearing his throat. "Normally adults are able to use the tunnels successfully. When we are teaching children to use them, we typically employ the buddy method. Maybe Mira could try with a buddy?" He asks, avoiding my gaze with the suggestion, remaining fixated on Vlad instead.

My cheeks heat, my mortification from the pool incident increasing with his comment. "Maybe I could watch some of my friends go first, then I can try again," I suggest. A small part of me secretly hopes someone else will mess up, to lessen the focus on my terrible performance thus far.

"Ahh, excellent suggestion Mira," Mr. Golden exclaims.

As a group we wander to the closest wall mounted travel tunnel. Each of my friends jumps in one at a time and of course, they all arrive safely at the tenth floor on their first try.

2

THE MAGIC

Mirabella

Two days later I develop a routine in Haven. After quickly braiding my golden locks, I slip into some comfortable clothes and exit my room into the hallway on the tenth floor, sliding the murky glass door behind me.

Looking down the hall, I notice the four doors leading to my friends' rooms are all still firmly shut. Their glass is lightly glowing, the magical way of indicating a room is occupied. Despite the late hour, it looks like I'm the first person awake.

Again.

With a resigned sigh, I wander down the white-walled hall towards the travel tunnel, attempting to mentally prepare myself for the journey to come. Upon reaching the tube, I begin my ritual. Eyes focused on the crystal-like, pink floors, I shake out my arms, then my legs, adding in a couple of deep, pre-birthing-like breaths, then I squeeze my eyes tightly shut. I jump inside repeating *four, four, four* in my mind, as loudly and often as possible.

Shortly after entering the tunnel, I'm shoved out by a small burst of powerful wind. My feet stumble slightly on the solid, pink floor beneath me. I regain my balance with my eyes still sealed tight, then slowly force my eyelids to separate once my feet feel stable underneath me.

A quick glance around confirms the dining hall is a few feet ahead and I release a deep, relieved breath at the sight.

I made it.

The travel tunnels have been one of the many culture shocks I've experienced since arriving in Haven, the city that resembles Candy Land. Not only does it have the appearance of another planet, it also operates like one.

Unlike Florence, Haven is so far on the outskirts of civilization, they make no attempts to tame the magic that runs rampant here. Anything that can be made more convenient with a spell, is. Most of the magical elements are greatly appreciated, but traveling by a magical system of pipes is taking some time to adjust to. The tubes intersect floors and even buildings, as a safe and efficient way to travel.

Supposedly.

I'm still getting a hang of the whole "jump into a mostly enclosed cylinder that leads many floors below and above you and think of your destination to travel there" thing. It's taken a few days for me to not scream every time I jump inside one. If there were any alternatives, I would not use the tubes... especially after the incident.

Shaking my head to return my thoughts to the present, I briskly enter the dining hall. I have big plans for the rest of my day, which don't include standing by myself and reliving my past embarrassments.

Instead, I step straight into a line of witches, waiting for spelled utensils to place desired food onto their plates. The line progresses quickly and within minutes, I'm exiting the line with a full plate. A brief scan of the tables shows no familiar faces. Although I expected as much, I still feel a slight pang of disappointment as I slip in a chair to eat breakfast by myself, again.

Focusing on my food, I devour my small pile of bacon and begin on my eggs. The sound of the chair to my left sliding out from under the table has my attention snapping in that direction. My eyes quickly meet a chest clad in a dark green button up. They travel up the form that has frozen under my scrutiny until they meet a pair of muddy brown eyes.

An angry scowl instantly replaces my curious expression. I throw my napkin onto my plate and begin to push back my chair. A set of large fingers grab my arm, halting my progress with a gentle but firm hold that locks me in place.

"Mira Love," Leif says, a strange expression marring his face. If a smirk could be contrite, a combination of guilt and smug superiority, that would describe Leif at this precise moment.

Without hesitation, I use a firm grip of my own and silently pry Leif's fingers away one by one. I back away from him and pick up my plate, prepared to make a hasty escape. My steps falter slightly when his whispered plea hits my ears. "Please, give me a chance. I know I messed up, but I need to speak with you... it's important."

My feet lock, as if super glued to the floor, like the only way to process his words is for my entire body to still. Leif takes advantage of my distraction, surging forward to close the scant distance between us.

His movement startles me, transporting me to a time, not too long ago, when he pretended to be someone else in order to throw me against a tree. My shoulders hunch and I curl my neck downward, an instinctive reaction intended to protect my face.

Leif notices the reaction and freezes. We both simultaneously step away from each other, creating a safe space between our bodies. Leif's signature smirk is nowhere to be found, and a concerned frown lightly mars his face. With his hands in front of him, he takes one slow step forward. "I'm so sorry, Mira Love..."

Shakily, I nod my head and reply without meeting

his eyes, "I appreciate your apology Leif, but it isn't enough. I don't know if anything will ever be enough for me to forgive you."

"This isn't about forgiveness, Mira Love. I need to warn..."

With an unsteady inhale, I silence Leif, by simply raising a single palm in the air. My eyes finally meet his, and unspoken words linger in the air heavily between us. Regret. Anger. Sadness. I trusted Leif, but he's broken my trust and I'm not stupid enough to offer it to him again so easily.

Thankfully, he's adept at reading my expression and allows me to walk away without causing a scene. I dump my dirty plate into a basin and leave the dining area with my head held high. Outwardly, I'm calm and collected, but inside my chest another small crack is added to the assortment crisscrossing my heart, one I'm not quite able to explain.

In the evening, I return to the tenth floor of Guest Building H feeling defeated and exhausted. I spent the majority of my day waiting for Archibald Golden to have a free space in his schedule, but he never did.

As I'm spit out of the travel tunnel, I glance down the hall. My gaze notes a row of dimmed, cloudy, pink doors, indicating the rest of my crew is still out in Haven somewhere instead of tucked safely inside their rooms. It's just after dinner time, so it isn't too surprising they aren't back yet, but I'm still left fighting a bone deep feeling of loneliness. My friends and I seem to have opposite schedules lately.

Sighing, I slide open the privacy glass leading to my room and immediately click on the lamp near my bed. The room is warm and small, with a diffuser scenting the air occasionally with light puffs of lavender and peppermint.

I inhale deeply before heading into the en-suite. Walking across the smooth, marble floor, which is pink of course, I turn the spigot to the tub, observing as the water steams while it pours out. The porcelain basin gradually fills, and I eye the assortment of bath powders on a shelf nearby, reaching forward to sample the smells before adding a floral scent to the water.

Sliding into the tub, I turn off the water and allow my brain to run free. It immediately jumps through every stress I've had over the past few months, which has been plenty. Thoughts flit between my most recent interaction with Leif, to missing my friends, to wondering about my parents, to fearing for the fate of the shifters.

Eventually I shut down the chaos with a singular, calming inhale. Counting to ten, I exhale a long stream of air and the tension drains from my shoulders as I focus on the heat of the water, the floral scent floating through the air, and the silence of the room.

Focusing on my surroundings calms my racing mind, as part of a meditative technique I've been working on. I found it in a text from the archives during my search for reference books that may contain a cure. So far, I have had little luck with curse-related texts. However, I found a book called "Tricks to Brewing Mastery" which contained tips and tricks to fine tune a witch's magic. I read the tome front to back in one sitting.

Most of the book was common sense. But the meditation technique, to focus on your spell and nothing else, seemed like something I should practice. Especially after studying with Leif for my witches exam and learning the direction of my thoughts can directly affect my witching abilities.

At this rather volatile time in my life, it's crucial I'm able to clear my mind and access my potion brewing at the drop of a hat. Therefore, meditation practice seemed like a good idea.

After another twenty minutes of soaking and intentional breathing, I unplug the drain and clamber out of the tub. Wrapping a fluffy robe around myself, I run a brush through my hair quickly, then reenter my bedroom.

My steps slow when I spot a familiar dark-haired form lounging across my bed. "Vlad," I exhale in a whisper, worried if I speak too loudly, I'll find his presence was a dream.

"Hey, little Mir," he says with a soft smile.

I hurry towards the bed, throwing myself forward when I'm inches away from the handsome guy that's felt like a stranger the last few days. Vlad catches me with strong, muscular arms, tucking me gently into his chest. His nose immediately finds the side of my neck and I feel his deep inhale.

"I haven't seen you in days," I murmur. Since arriving in Haven, my friends have been rather absent. Their schedules haven't matched up with mine. I know because their doors show they rise later than me and return to their rooms, long after I've gone to bed.

"Yeah, it does feel that way. What have you been up to?" Vlad asks, his words muffled as he speaks against my hair.

A feeling of incredulousness floods my veins. Is he serious?

I attempt to pull away, but Vlad's heavy arms have me trapped, holding me tightly against his body. I'm forced to speak without making eye contact with the amber orbs I know are hovering above my head. "I've been waiting for a meeting with the Coven Leader and researching in the archives. You know, just pursuing the mission we came here for, looking for a cure for the shifters..."

"Oh, I forgot." Vlad murmur, his voice sounding groggy, as if sleep is closing in.

He... forgot?

I wriggle from Vlad's hold, forcing his thick arms away from my body. We need to continue this conversation face to face. He doesn't relax his arms in the slightest, but I eventually break free from his grip.

With a deep breath, I look into Vlad's eyes, only to find the amber orbs are sealed shut. Groaning, I realize somehow, even with all my jostling, Vlad has fallen asleep. With a huff, I lay back down on my side and am quickly swept back into his chest.

Even while sleeping, he wants to be close. The thought helps to ease a portion of my annoyance, and I allow his warmth and ocean-pine scent to comfort me, lulling me into a state of half-consciousness.

We'll have time to talk more tomorrow.

3

THE DISAPPOINTMENT

Mirabella

I wake naturally as the first rays of sunlight hit my window, seeping into my room and illuminating my otherwise empty bed. The spot Vlad was sleeping in is cold, so I assume he left in the middle of the night to avoid being caught. Although it doesn't seem like anyone would come to check on us, or even care if Vlad was in my room.

Forcing myself from bed, I begin the process of getting ready for another day of waiting to speak with Archibald Golden and searching the archives. Dressed in a pair of skinny jeans, and a bright, floral top, I exit into the hallway. Glancing to my right, I see the rest of my crew's doors still glowing. Including Vlad's.

Sighing, I stroll towards the travel tunnels, alone as

usual. Inhaling a deep breath, I hop in with both feet locked together thinking *Coven Leader's Office* on repeat. I'm shoved out of the tunnel with a burst of air and barely catch my footing before landing face first on the carpet of Archibald Golden's reception area.

Like the other days I've waited in the lobby, the expansive space is bereft of other occupants beside Archibald Golden's receptionist, Lena. I approach Lena's desk, like I always do, and paste a kind smile on my face. "Hi, does Mr. Golden have any appointments available to speak with me today?"

She releases an exasperated exhale. "He can see you in five more days. I have you on Archibald's calendar then for a ten o'clock meeting. His schedule is remarkably busy, and he cannot accept last minute appointments." She says this all without looking up from her computer, her fingers flying across the keyboard at a rapid pace.

I examine her crisp white button up, small round glasses and dark hair pulled into a loose chignon. She looks exactly the same every day I've been here, as if she has a closet full of the same shirts and only knows one hairstyle.

Fighting to contain my huff, I drag my eyes away from Lena and trudge to one of the chairs lining the room. I plop down with an angry exhale. As a distraction, I fiddle with my phone, attempting to keep my mind busy while I wait. It lasts about seven seconds before my eyes begin to wander from pure boredom.

The Coven Leader's reception area is the only room I've seen so far that isn't pink. It boasts plush, dark green carpet with wood paneled walls. The desk Lena sits behind is a wooden monstrosity, made of darkened pine. Everything seems to be a direct contrast to the pink and gold accents that decorate the rest of Haven. It looks like a gentlemen's cigar lounge versus a reception area.

My eyes continue to rove the room while my thoughts wander. No one exits or enters Mr. Golden's office in the time I sit there. My plan was to intercept him and woo him into a meeting with my urgent pleas, but that doesn't seem likely to happen today.

Sighing, I aim a glare at Lena. I'm suspicious she's lying about Mr. Golden's packed schedule, but lack any way to prove it, short of outright accusation. Pushing off the arms of the chair, I rise to my feet and prepare to leave.

"Bye Lena, see you tomorrow," I call out as I near the travel tunnel. She waves but doesn't speak or raise her eyes from the computer screen. Her steady clicks on the keyboard accompany me as I jump in, feet first.

THE PAST FEW DAYS, I've immediately gone to the archives, following my visit to the Coven Leader's office. Today, however, I decide to search for my friends. We haven't seen much of each other lately, and I'm curious what they've been up to.

Trusting the magic of the travel tunnels, I jump in with both feet and think *take me to my friends.*

The wind ramps up in the tube and whisks me away. Within seconds I'm shot outwards in a burst of air, stumbling to catch my footing without registering my surroundings.

My feet finally steady and my eyes pop open to find I've landed on a familiar platform. It extends a couple dozen feet ahead of me, ending a mere eighth of the way into the cavernous square room with clean white walls and a ceiling made of skylights.

About twenty feet below the platform, a burgundy colored net spans from wall to wall. Nothing appears to connect it to the walls, so it must be magicked into place. My brief observation of the room ends with a few kids practicing on the blue hover discs. Their balance is rather precarious, but they're probably doing better than I would.

With a sigh, I turn to reenter the travel tunnel. This is the second time it's brought me here. Although this time the tunnel dropped me on the platform, at least. I'm starting to think it's some type of prank. Maybe Leif programmed the tubes to sporadically drop me here whenever I think about anything besides a specific room or floor.

I inhale deeply, preparing to hop back into the tube. I take two steps forward when a familiar cackling laugh hits my ears. The noise is quickly followed by an equally familiar rumbling laugh. Twirling around, I suddenly spot Vlad's broad shouldered form and Sylvia's shock of bright violet hair. The two are on blue discs swooping down from the ceiling towards the kids unsteadily floating above the net.

My hand flies to my mouth, like a concerned parent, when Sylvia heads straight towards a young boy that appears to barely be able to maintain an upright position. At the last second, she swerves aggressively to avoid him, but the wind from her movement knocks him over and he drops onto the net.

Vlad swoops over to the platform, smoothly jumping from his disc to stand next to me. "Little Mir," he rumbles happily. "I never see you anymore. Are you here to come practice hover discing with us?" After he finishes speaking, he steps forward and buries his nose in my hair while wrapping his thick arms around me.

Despite my fury, I nestle into his grip, leaning my cheek lightly against his chest. Before I speak, I inhale a few deep, calming breaths. I feel my rage transition into irritation and wait a few more beats to ensure I don't cause a scene in front of all these kids.

Once I have control over my emotions, I step free of Vlad's hold. "Yeah, you never seem to be around," I reply in a clipped tone.

Sylvia hovers closer and snags my attention with a wave and a cheery grin. My eyes flit from her to Vlad as I grit out, "Both of you are supposed to be here to help me. Here to help the shifters. I thought you were searching for answers on your own, but it looks like you've just been messing around all day. Have you done anything besides this?"

The sunny smile on Sylvia's face drops into a frown. Her gaze flits between Vlad and I briefly, then she responds, "I don't know anything about a cure, but this conversation is so boring." She flies closer to the platform and jabs Vlad in the arm with a single finger. She skits her hover disc further away and calls over her shoulder, "Bet I can beat you to the top!"

Sylvia zips off, soaring diagonally towards the ceiling at a treacherous angle. Her feet are braced with her shoulders hunched close to her board. She appears to know what she's doing, but the sight of her sailing through the air still creates a pang of anxiety.

Please don't let her get hurt.

Out of the corner of my eye, I spot Vlad leaping off the platform and onto his disc. He angles himself at an equally steep incline, chasing after Sylvia while rapidly gaining speed.

My previous concern amplifies while I watch, waiting for them to turn around and come back. In my mind, they're both seconds away from returning to the platform to say, "Just kidding. How can we help, Mira?"

Seconds turn into minutes. My gaze traces Vlad and Sylvia as they reach the top of the room, each of them tapping a palm against the paned windows comprising the ceiling. Then they dive to the bottom of the room to twist and wind their way through the remaining hover discers.

Are you freaking kidding me?

My previous concern over their well-being morphs into anger. I swallow the rage-scream building in my throat, barely.

Instead of shrieking like a banshee, I focus on taking another set of deep, meditative breaths. I spin on my heel and jump into the travel tunnel thinking, *take me to Marc and Alex Sieves.*

Maybe they've been more productive than playing juvenile racing games all day.

I'm spit into a gigantic space with concrete floors and mostly blank walls. Glancing around, I spot couches shaped in a U around a television, pinball machines, and an air hockey table. After my brief inspection, I deduce this is some sort of rec room.

Stepping away from the travel tunnel, a flash of golden hair catches my attention. I walk to the left until I reach a large, square ring that looks like it's used for boxing matches. In the center of the ring, the twins are leaping at each other, throwing punches, and ducking away. Their bare feet weave and dance across the surface of the floor and I become entranced in their graceful movements.

I didn't know the twins knew how to fight.

"We don't!" Alex exclaims, barely avoiding a punch from his brother after a quick glance in my direction.

I realize I spoke the thought aloud when Marc

adds, "We found a potion to gain fighting skills." He stops bouncing on his toes, and points to a table stationed against the wall. "That book has all sorts of fun and interesting things in it."

His momentary distraction gives Alex the advantage and he socks him straight in the nose. Marc goes down with an audible thud, his hands both grasping his face. I gasp, looking around for something to help.

Running to the table with the manual, I grab a towel off the top of a stack near the end. I jog back to the ring and yank the rope sides apart to clamber inside. I reach Marc at the same time as Alex. He offers his twin a vial of vibrant blue liquid, which Marc sips without question.

In seconds, the blood stops flowing from his face and he slowly stands as he heals. Two sets of emerald eyes glance in my direction. I silently offer the towel while my blood boils.

Is this what the twins have been doing the entire time we've been here?

Silently, I leave the ring and return to the table. I flip the potion manual closed, my eyes skim over the cover. I read, "Sports Magic 101." Scoffing, I stomp towards the travel tunnel. The twins haven't been searching for a cure either.

"Mira!"

The call of my name stops me, and I feel some tension in my shoulders drain. Preparing to receive an apology, I straighten my features and pivot on my heel, meeting Alex's animated emerald gaze.

"Do you want to come join us? We could use a third person to spice up the competition. It's like playing a video game, only better."

My neutral expression quickly morphs into incredulity. Have my friends lost their freaking minds?

I must say the words out loud because Marc responds to me, "I don't think so. But do you want in or not? Alex and I are tied right now and it would be nice to have some fresh meat in the game!"

My gaze flits from Marc to Alex, then back to Marc again. Inhaling a deep breath and quirking a brow, I ask, "Does fighting have a secret connection to finding the cure for the shifters? Out of everyone here, I thought you two would be the most invested, since one of you was just recently cured and all."

Marc's brow furrows as he thinks. After a pause, he finally replies, "I don't really know what you're talking about, Mira. But you're kind of killing the vibe down here. You should either drink the potion or go be unfun somewhere else."

A pang of hurt clatters through my chest. What is going on with my friends? I thought we were a team. When we left Florence, it was like a big "One for All, All for One" moment, but being in Haven, I feel more alone than I ever have before.

With a heavy heart, I wordlessly turn from the

twins and amble towards the travel tunnel. Sighing, I jump into the tube with both feet connected. It takes a second for me to remember I need a destination in mind. I barely have time to form a thought as I hit the cyclone with my eyes screwed shut and am carried away.

4

THE ARCHIVES

Mirabella

I leave my friends to their shenanigans, barely remembering to think my destination as I hit the wind of the travel tunnel. I force the word *Archives* to run through my mind on repeat, hoping to avoid another incident, despite the delay.

When I'm spit from the tube, I cautiously open my eyes, scanning my surroundings with awe. Regardless of the amount of time I spend down here, the archives never fail to impress me. The entrance is large and circular, like a giant bank vault door, consisting of the same pink crystal that distinguishes the rest of Haven. Although the sight is architecturally beautiful, the real prize is beyond the crystal, tucked just out of sight.

Past the vault door is a nine-story structure. The center is open, like an atrium. If you stand in the very middle and look upwards, you can see wall upon wall, completely lined with books. Each floor has dozens of bookshelves coated in ancient tomes.

Pushing aside my hurt from earlier, I walk to the entrance, pausing just under the circular entry. I inhale a deep breath, basking in the smells associated with new and old books. The scent of knowledge.

I wind my way across the bottom floor, weaving in and out of the randomly placed shelves and tables, until I reach the middle. Stopping near my usual table, I crane my neck back, my eyes sliding across the leather-bound covers varying in every shape, size, and color imaginable.

The sight helps to rid me of my foul mood, replacing my heartbroken frustration with excitement. Even if my friends are acting strangely, I'm still grateful for the opportunity to be in Haven and search the archives for answers.

My eyes follow a historian as he or she replaces books on the shelves of the seventh story. The archives are staffed by fully robed individuals that assist visitors with finding books on the upper levels. Rather quickly, I discovered only the main floor of the archives is open to guests.

Plopping into my usual spot, I snag a book from across the table, left from the day prior. I slide it towards me and flip open the cover, anxious to get started. A part of me hopes that if I find something useful and bring it to my friends, they'll snap out of whatever weird funk they've fallen into.

A historian passes my table sometime later and I tap their arm gently, signifying I need additional assistance. "Can I get the next batch of books?" I ask, in a hushed tone.

Since I wasn't sure where to start, I just asked for any books detailing the history of shifters. Apparently, the archives contain a surprising number of texts on the topic, because the historians have been bringing groups of twenty. When I was preparing to leave after the first batch, I was wordlessly stopped and more books were brought on a floating cart and swapped with the ones they previously provided me. Several more batches of books have arrived since then, and there doesn't appear to be an end in sight.

The historian lingering nearby offers a brusque nod in response to my request. Swishes of their robes signify their retreat and my eyes trace the figure, leaving with a straight spine and purposeful steps. I watch until they're out of sight.

Reluctantly, I return to the volume I've been reading for the past few hours. I flip through the last remaining pages and close the book with an audible thud. A feeling of defeat tries to well in my chest, but I tamp it down, forcing it into the rapidly filling box I've shoved all of my negative emotions into the last few days. Once it's locked away, I take a few meditative breaths, closing my eyes to count to ten.

When I reopen them, I glance around the library and find no one else is around to use as a distraction. I pull over the notepad left by a historian on a previous day and begin to lightly drag a pen across the blank surface.

The page rapidly fills with outlines, and slowly the shapes take form. Within minutes, I have a rough black and white sketch completed. Placing the pen on the table, I lift the pad of paper in my hands and lean back in my chair while I scan the image.

It's clearly a depiction of the archives, which isn't too surprising considering I've spent so much of my free time here recently. What is strange, however, is a blurred ball in the center of the page. It appears to be slamming against the side of a bookshelf. The image looks like a snapshot in time, just as one of the bookcases is being impacted and slowly tilting backwards, about to hit the one behind it. Although it can't be seen in my drawing, the closeness of the bookshelves would clearly cause a ripple effect, leading another to fall shortly after the first two.

Well, that would be terrible.

Not wanting to get caught with an image depicting imminent destruction of Haven's archives, I scribble over my picture and shove the pad of paper back to the far side of the table. The historian returns with a cart crammed full of texts the second the pad stops moving.

They silently swap the tomes, waiting to the left of my chair for any additional requests. Despite my less than stellar search thus far, I offer a warm smile and murmur, "Thank you for your help. This is everything I need."

The historian's face isn't visible past the long hood of their robe. He, or she, simply nods in response, then leaves me to the hunt.

One of the books on the table captures my attention. It has a deep, forest green leather binding that reminds me of the fir trees lining Vlad's backyard. I snatch it up first, opening to a random page without skimming the title.

The first word I read says "Legacy". At first, I think I found another book about legacy witches, like the one Leif showed me in my parents' witching chamber. I'm seconds away from closing the book and moving on, assuming it was accidentally added to my stack, when the word "shifters" catches my eye. My gaze flits over the page and slowly widens in shock.

This is a book about shifter legacies.

Voices suddenly start echoing through the library, breaking my concentration. Straining my ears, I faintly hear noise filtering in from the entry. Curiosity has me rising to my feet and striding in the sound's direction. I clutch the book tightly to my chest as if it will disappear if I release it. I'm not sure what the text contains, but in my bones, I feel it is important.

As I approach the entrance, the noises become distinguishable as the voices of my friends. My shoulders fill with tension and I pick up my pace, hoping to intercept them before they cause any trouble.

"Little Mir."

"Mira!"

"Mir, where are you?"

I round a corner and immediately smack into Sylvia. The two of us bounce apart and I fall backwards onto the floor. An "oomph" flies from my lips and one of my hands cups my nose, which I believe Sylvia may have broken with her unreasonably hard shoulder bone as it has begun throbbing.

The pain quickly lessens and I prod the appendage to ensure it's not broken, while maintaining a death grip on the legacy book. Once I'm sure my nose isn't bleeding or broken, I glance up, just in time to watch Sylvia hop to her feet and brush off her bum.

"Oh, there you are, Mira," she says in a perky tone.

She offers a hand to help me up. I eye it hesitantly for a second, before grabbing on and using the leverage to pull myself to my feet.

"Here I am," I reply in a dead tone, once I'm upright.

I want to add *like I have been every day since we arrived, while you were too busy fooling around with my boyfriend to help me,* but I don't want to sound too bitter if she's finally here to offer to help.

Looking past Sylvia, I see Vlad and the twins are here too. My entire rag-tag crew, reunited.

A part of me wonders if they found all the magic in

Haven way more exciting than I did, and just needed a few days to explore it before they were ready to work. Hope blossoms and I quickly shed my bad attitude. A grin splits my face and I pivot, facing the direction I came from.

"Ready?" I ask, throwing the words over my shoulder.

"Uh, for what?" Vlad returns.

Confused, I twirl back around. "Aren't you here to help me search the archives?"

"Search the archives?" Alex asks. "Is that what you've been doing down here? Playing hide and seek?"

"Uhm, no," I reply, hesitantly. "I've been searching the books for clues on how to cure the curse affecting witches and shifters. You know, the thing we all agreed to do together when we left Florence to come here..." I trail off once I realize no one is listening.

My eyebrows draw together at the scene unfolding before me. Sylvia has randomly acquired chalk, even though she has no pockets on her person. She's using a thick piece to draw a game of uneven hopscotch squares on the floor.

I need to address that problem soon, but I find my gaze pulled to Vlad. He's lounging against a bookcase, pouting. I'm bewildered by his behavior as he transitions from a full-on duck face to a seductive half smile. He winks at an imaginary audience, straightening to pop a hip and place his hand in his back pocket. Vlad looks good in his dark denim jeans, and fitted white T, but this is a whole new level of weird. It's almost like he's imagining himself at a photo shoot.

A sudden shout sounds from the area behind me. Shaking my head, I spin one-hundred and eighty degrees and hone in on Marc and Alex swatting at each other.

Another yell echoes across the archives as Marc angrily insists, "No, I'm first."

"No, me. I'm older." Alex screams.

As if in slow motion, I watch Marc shove Alex, pushing him towards one of the towering bookcases nearby. I lunge forward, yelling, "No!"

I'm too far away, and the damage has already been done. Before I can stop it, the dual weight of the twin's impact, or maybe Marc's shifter strength, topples the entire bookshelf backwards. It tilts, then wobbles back, like maybe it can right itself, but unfortunately, it isn't able to and dips backwards once more.

A gasp leaves my lips, as the worst version of dominos unfolds before my eyes. The bookcase hits the center shelf of the unit behind it. The noise of splintering wood echoes across the archives, forever imprinting itself on my brain as the chaos continues.

The second shelf repeats the motion of the first, wobbling slightly, but ultimately tipping backwards until it smashes into the shelf behind it. The fourth shelf doesn't stand a chance, immediately smashing into the fifth.

A tear seeps from the corner of my eye as I watch

on in horror. The destruction feels like it takes hours, but it's likely only minutes. That's all it takes for half of the bottom level of the archives to be decimated, leaving broken wood and ripped books strewn across the ground like the remnants of a horrific battle.

I shut my eyes, sending up a small prayer in case anyone is listening. *Please, please let this not be real.*

The sound of hands clapping together, combined with an excited squeal has my eyes popping open once more. Unfortunately, the scene remains unchanged. The twins are slowly rising to their feet amidst the rubble and I pivot to look at the rest of my group.

My eyes land on Sylvia and she exclaims, "That was amazing! Let's do it again!"

As the words leave her lips, a historian approaches us. A stern, loud voice booms out of the robed face, "You." An arm raises, the draping fabric of the robe aimed toward me and my supposed friends. "Leave and do not come back."

I open my mouth to protest, then snap my jaw shut. After the absolute mayhem caused by my friends, I agree they need to leave and should never be allowed back. I don't want to argue on their behalf, so for now, I'll leave too.

Hopefully, during my meeting with Archibald Golden, I can convince him to allow me, and only me, back into the archives to continue my research.

Clinging onto that hope, I consider what to do with the legacy shifter book. I don't know when, or even if,

I'll be allowed to return, and I feel it in my gut that this book has information that I need. In a split-second decision, I shimmy the book into my pants, wrapping my arms around my belly to help keep it hidden.

The historian remains a menacing presence standing over our group, with a raised arm directing us to the exit. Despite the strange behavior of my friends recently, they appear to understand the gravity of the situation and quickly file out of the archives. I waddle behind them, fighting the waves of disappointment, confusion, and rage that are threatening to overwhelm me at any moment.

The second we exit the vault shaped door, Alex stops abruptly. His emerald gaze connects with mine and he offers a tiny smile. Expecting an apology, I return the expression. He opens his mouth and asks, "Are you free to have fun now?"

It takes a second for his words to process, but once they do, a white-hot rage builds, causing my blood to boil. My fury bursts free with my next words. "No, I'm not free to *have fun,*" I state, my tone mocking the cadence of his. "And you shouldn't be either."

I pause, my gaze scanning the group. "I thought everyone understood we were here on a mission. We need to find a cure, clear my name, and restore the shifters. Since we've arrived, you have all been acting like children and I don't understand why. Does anyone care to explain their sudden lack of interest in helping our friends and family?"

My furious words echo around the chamber as Alex, Marc, Sylvia, and Vlad exchange stunned looks. No one responds, or makes any move to apologize, and the silence stretches into an uncomfortable length of time.

Throwing my hands up in the air, I stomp past them. Leaping into the travel tunnel, I think *my room* and leave my "friends" behind.

5

THE DECEPTION

Mirabella

I step from my bath, dripping water and seething anger from earlier. When we left Florence, it was apparent our mission was to help the wolves. Anyone who wasn't invested should have stayed behind. To my relief, everyone jumped through the portal after me, pledging their allegiance to my cause.

Or so I thought.

Other than the commitment they made at that moment, to leave Florence with someone being hunted by the coven, my supposed friends have done nothing to help. While I've been tearing through books and awaiting the elusive Archibald Golden, the rest of my group has been learning how to use hover discs and pretending to be MMA fighters.

Then, they bring their antics to the archives and ruin the only hope we have for finding answers.

Like, are you freaking kidding me?

I grumble aloud at the thought, then wrap the robe from the back of my door around my body. When I re-enter the bedroom, I'm greeted by a lanky, golden-haired form leaning against my door. My sour mood instantly worsens.

"Mira Love," he says. He's lounging with an easy-going expression, like he has a right to be in my room.

"Leif, get out," I respond with a huff. Preparing for the inevitable argument to come, I square my shoulders and pull the edges of my robe tighter around my body. I need to bring clothes into the bathroom with me, since everyone seems to ignore the glowing door indicator and forgo knocking to enter without permission.

"I will," he promises, straightening slightly. "I'm not here for anything... untoward." The word causes a glimmer of a smirk, but he quickly flattens his lips against the expression.

His sternness piques my curiosity. At least that's what I tell myself when I decide not to shove him out the door immediately.

Sighing, I perch on the edge of my bed, shimmying my robe back into place when the front threatens to gape open. Once settled, I return my gaze to Leif's. "I'm listening."

He remains near the wall, but stands fully,

extending his lanky limbs. His mouth is set in a grim line and his brow is slightly furrowed like he's unsure how to begin. "Look I'm sorry about what happened before. I've tried to apologize at least a dozen times since you've been here, but you keep brushing me off." I open my mouth to respond, but he rushes to continue before I have a chance to speak. "For good reason, I understand that. I'm not just here to apologize, I have important information to tell you. I don't know where to start exactly, but it's about your friends and the curse."

A frown mars my face. "Start at the beginning," I reply firmly.

Leif nods, his brow flattening as he speaks. "When I returned home, my father wasn't... pleased." He pauses, but I don't fill the silence.

I need Leif to tell me why he's here, or get out.

"He was one of the driving forces behind me asking you to move here and join my coven. My father has always told my sister and I that the most important way to honor our legacy is to find powerful witches and marry them. It keeps our bloodlines, and our coven, strong. When he heard of another legacy witch needing help... he didn't hesitate to send me, hoping we would hit it off."

An unidentifiable emotion flares to life as my brain slowly processes the meaning of his words. Leif's dad sent him to Florence with a distinct mission in mind. Archibald Golden heard a legacy witch needed help and sent his son in response. Hoping by some chance of fate we would find a connection that would eventually lead to marriage and "carrying on their strong bloodline".

My cheeks heat as a result of the fury and embarrassment that simmers just beneath the surface of my skin. Unfortunately, or maybe fortunately, I'm not given much time to continue down that rabbit hole. Leif has finally hit his stride and is intent on finishing his story.

"When I came home without you, my father was… very disappointed. I was able to appease him with the idea of your imminent arrival. I was banking on you coming here for help to solve the curse affecting the shifters." He stops speaking, his muddy gaze fixated on mine.

Leif's weighted stare combined with the heavy silence filling the room becomes uncomfortable. Hoping to alleviate some tension, I make a "go on" gesture with my hand to encourage him to finish his story. His lengthy silences are similar to my grandmother's and it's wearing on my patience.

Thankfully, he takes the hint.

"My father wants you to stay here in Haven. His goal is to have the strongest coven in the world and he wants to accumulate as many legacy witches as possible to make that reality. The fact that you have at least one other legacy witch in your party has him giddy beyond belief." My brow furrows at the words 'one other legacy witch', but Leif continues unperturbed by my expression, "What I'm trying to get at, is he's put measures in place to keep you and your friends here, forever."

"What type of measures?" I ask hesitantly as the ominous meaning of Leif's words seep into my consciousness.

Leif stares at me when he questions back, "Have your friends been acting strangely since you've arrived in Haven? Do they appear to no longer care about saving the shifters?"

My eyes widen as I recall my previous conversation with Vlad, when he said he forgot about the shifters. Following our talk, he and the rest of my friends have done nothing but fool around and cause chaos to include the most recent incident in the archives.

How did Leif know?

As soon as the thought crosses my mind, I become instantly suspicious. This is Leif, after all, and he's already proven he doesn't always have my best interests at heart.

"What do you know?" I ask, attempting to keep accusation from seeping into my tone.

He suddenly strides across the room, halting next to my nightstand near the head of my bed. "Do you know what this is?" He asks, picking up the diffuser that's been scenting my room with a heady peppermint and lavender aroma.

"A diffuser..." I respond, wondering about the random change in topic.

Leif nods. "Yes, and in the witching world they can slow release potions into the air, in order to lengthen the effects of the magic."

I remain silent, still unsure where this conversation is heading.

"I've been coming into your room every afternoon and replacing an apathy potion loaded into your diffuser with lavender and peppermint oil."

I gasp when his words register. "An apathy potion? What does that do? Where has it been coming from?"

"It causes forgetfulness and makes those under its effects shirk their responsibilities for tasks they perceive as 'fun'. If used correctly, it helps reduce stress and anxiety, but if under the effects long term, people lose their motivation and ability to focus."

"Why have you been helping me? How did you know?" I shoot off rapid fire questions, not sure I want to believe Leif.

The internal struggle only lasts a few seconds. Despite his actions in Florence, Leif's words describe the recent actions of my friends. There really isn't any other way to explain their behavior since we arrived in Haven.

I don't know if it's wise to trust Leif... but I do.

As if he can sense my wavering trust, he holds his hands in the air before him, to pacify me. "Look, I haven't always been a nice guy or made the right decisions, but I want to break the curse. As a witch, I have skin in the game too, eh?"

I weigh his words, his answers creating more questions as I mull them over. "Why didn't you tell me this sooner? And why have you only been replacing the potion in my room?"

Leif shrugs, lounging back against the door once more. "I couldn't replace all the potions. My father would become suspicious if none of them were working and your entire group continued to search for answers. Like I said before, I've been trying to get your attention since you arrived and you kept brushing me off. If you would have spoken with me sooner, I would have told you..."

He trails off like there's nothing else to say. And maybe there isn't. His words have revealed the perpetrator behind my friend's actions and I have officially exhausted all my patience with Archibald Golden.

I move towards my door, and Leif takes a step forward, opening his arms as if expecting a hug. Pushing past him, I slide the cloudy crystal door to the left and gesture at the hallway silently.

Surprisingly, Leif exits without protest. He must realize my issues are with a different Golden now.

I storm into the Head of Coven's reception area and ignore Lena's protests as I march straight to Mr. Golden's office. Grabbing the handle to the stupidly huge door, I yank it open. My conviction falters at the sight that greets me and I stop dumbfounded in the entryway.

The incredibly prestigious, unbelievably busy Archibald Golden is playing... golf.

He's standing near the edge of the room next to what appears to be a large, rectangular wall cut out that spans floor to ceiling. The city of Haven is visible to the sides, but the ground directly below the window is an expanse of grass, bordered by fir trees.

As I stand in the doorway watching him, Mr. Golden lifts his club in the air, arcing it behind his back. He pauses momentarily before swinging it forward towards the ground. My eyes barely skim across the floor, noting a golf ball seconds prior to his golf club connecting with it. An audible clacking noise sounds as he makes contact, sending the ball sailing out the cutout to land somewhere in the grass below.

Indignation blooms in my chest as he replaces the ball and repeats the motion, entirely oblivious to my presence. THIS is the reason Mr. Golden was too busy to meet with me the last few days. He was playing golf in his office.

I huff, signifying my annoyance, right as Mr. Golden releases his swing. His head swivels in my direction as his club sails through the air, missing the ball entirely.

"Miss Love?" He asks, his brow furrowed in confusion as he rests his golf club against the wall next to the open space. "I didn't realize we were set to meet today.

My calendar must not have been up to date." His words are casual, as is his stance, with his hands placed in the pockets of his checkered purple and green golf pants. Despite his relaxed demeanor, his shoulders are tight with tension and his eyes are wary.

The expression solidifies my belief in Leif. His father is doing something to my friends, and he's been avoiding me because his goal is to keep us here.

I waver momentarily, my eyes locked onto the vibrant blue orbs of Archibald Golden as I decide how to play this. I didn't exactly form a comprehensive plan before storming in here. I was fueled by indignant rage. As my anger diminishes slightly, I'm regretting my decision to arrive without plans or even backup.

Squaring my shoulders, I choose to be straightforward. "Why are you using an apathy potion on my friends?"

Mr. Golden lifts a hand from his pocket to scratch his chin. His bright blue gaze never leaves mine and I see a number of emotions flit across their clear surface. He finally stops scratching and his expression immediately shutters, the previously expressive blue orbs becoming emotionless.

The transition is so startling, I'm forced to lock my knees to remain in place. All I want to do is run for the hills, my body is practically pulsing with the urge to do so.

"You're a very intelligent young woman, Miss Love. One I do not think your coven gives enough credit to."

As he speaks, Mr. Golden straightens and prowls across the room. The motion is so predatory, the hairs on my arms raise in warning, urging me to leave while I still can.

Ignoring the feeling, I ask, "What do you mean?"

Mr. Golden chuckles and this time I'm unable to stop myself from stepping backwards. The sound is chilling.

Noticing my stunted movement, he pauses his advance and states, "They assumed they could stop you from passing your witches exams, which would force you to study more and drop the idea of helping the wolves. When that didn't work, they assumed you wouldn't find answers and would give up."

He shakes his head like the idea was ludicrous. "From what little Leif told me about you, I knew that wouldn't be the case. After you ran from your coven, they warned me you would come here, as did Leif. I assured the Northwest Coven that I would detain and distract you, but it appears even I have underestimated you and your pursuit of the 'Cure', Miss Love."

My heart rate speeds up as my brain slowly processes his words. The Coven has been trying to keep me away from the wolves? They sabotaged my witches exams? Thoughts are pinging through my mind so quickly, I barely have time to consider one idea before moving on to the next.

My blood pounds in my ears and I feel lightheaded as revelations hit me one after another. Inhaling deeply, I count to ten as I release all the air in my lungs. I repeat the act twice more and finally feel my pulse returning to normal.

Shaking my head to clear it, I murmur, "Why?"

I half-expect Mr. Golden to pretend he didn't hear me, so I'm slightly surprised when he responds, "The accelerated decline of the shifters signifies the end of the curse. Can't you see? If the witches saved them, the curse would continue for eternity. The death of their race is the only way to restore our magic."

A gasp escapes my lips and Mr. Golden begins to laugh maniacally. Part of my brain recognizes this man is clearly unhinged and urges my feet to move. Following my instinct, I sprint from the room towards the travel tunnels.

I've never run faster in my life.

Archibald Golden's insane laughter echoes around me as I enter the lobby. I continue to sprint away, each foot barely touching the ground before lifting again, in an effort to escape.

6

THE DEPARTURE

Mirabella

I stumble from the travel tunnel, continuing to surge forward without allowing myself time to secure my footing. My unsteady steps carry me closer to my room and I send up a small prayer, in case anyone is listening. *Please let my friends be in their rooms for once.*

Unfortunately, no one seems to be granting my requests today. When I glance down the hall, none of the doors belonging to my crew are lit with the magical occupancy indicator.

Groaning, I shove against my door, sliding it open so hard, it bounces back to a halfway closed position. I shoulder past it, my mind already on the next task, but pull up short when I notice my room is heavily occupied.

Leif's back is facing me as he stands sentry to the door leading into the hall. Beyond his lanky frame, Alex, Marc, Sylvia, and Vlad are sitting on my bed. Their gazes are fixated on something laying across the center of the comforter.

Stepping in further, I slide the door closed. A high-pitched voice singing a childish melody instantly captures my attention. A laugh bubbles up my throat as I realize the sound is coming from a movie playing on a tablet. Leif was able to hold my friends captive with a movie about trolls.

At the sound of the latch clicking shut, Leif's gaze connects with mine, while the rest of the group remains focused on the show. A twinkle of amusement glints in his brown eyes, like he's as tickled by the situation as I am. My lips automatically form a grin in response, prior to remembering Leif isn't exactly my friend.

Glancing away, I whisper, "What's going on?"

Leif responds with a question, "Did you confront my father?" Startled, my gaze returns to his. "I know you, Mira Love. Even if you're mad at me and wish to pretend I don't."

My eyes narrow and Leif sighs like he's utterly exhausted. "Very well. If you confronted my father, we need to escape from Haven, immediately. All of us need to. My father doesn't like to be trifled with, and I can guarantee he'll lock you away until he convinces you to stay in Haven, permanently. He has ways to bend you to his will."

I grimace, but I'm honestly not too surprised by his words. Mr. Golden doesn't seem entirely stable. Not if his revelations are any indication, anyway. Full body chills consume me as I take a moment to think over the ramifications of his confessions.

Mr. Golden, and the rest of the witching community, are against a cure for the shifters. My friends and I are the only ones searching for a cure. A gasp leaves my lips as the thoughts slot into place for the first time.

We need to leave as soon as possible.

"What do we do about them?" I whisper, gesturing towards my friends at the same second Marc shoves Alex off the bed.

"Hey! Why did you push me?" Alex cries, remaining on the floor.

"You were singing over the tablet and I couldn't hear," Marc returns with a shrug.

"Be nice or I'll take the tablet away. Hands to yourself," Leif calmly instructs, as if settling arguments between grown men acting like they're five is an everyday occurrence for him. Honestly, with his crazy father, maybe it is.

Leif faces me again and offers a hand. Nestled inside his palm is a thin vial filled with clear liquid. "They each need a sip of this. It will clear the effects of an unwanted potion."

I nod, uncorking the vial and taking a tiny sniff,

hoping for a hint as to what it contains. The liquid is odorless, however.

The idea of offering some unknown potion to my friends concerns me. I waver briefly before deciding I have little choice. When it comes to trusting our fate with Leif or Mr. Golden, I will certainly choose the former.

Squaring my shoulders, I solidify my decision by entering the bathroom and snagging a clear, plastic cup off the counter. I return to the bed and approach Vlad first, pouring a sip worth of the potion into the empty cup.

"Drink this if you want to keep watching the movie," I state firmly.

Vlad's eyes never leave the tablet. He snags the cup from my hand, nearly knocking it over in his haste to gulps down the liquid. I remain standing in front of him, crossing my fingers and fervently hoping it works.

Within seconds, Vlad's entire demeanor changes. His shoulders tense as his gaze lifts from the tablet, immediately catching on Leif. Locked on him, he rises from the bed and grabs onto my biceps. He shoves me behind him, using one hand to keep me in place. I can no longer see his expression, but a deep menacing growl, issued from the back of his throat conveys his feelings.

Crap.

Tension radiates off him and I immediately grow concerned he's seconds away from shifting into a massive, furry beast. If it comes to that, there will be no reasoning with him.

"Vlad," I plead, gently stroking down his spine with three of my fingertips, hoping to gain his attention.

The growling lessens with the movement, but he doesn't face me. Pushing away his bent arm, locking me in place, I slide around his body. With both palms on his chest, I tip my head backwards, attempting to connect with his amber gaze, "Vlad."

He finally tears his eyes away from Leif, and we simultaneously sway forward. Vlad presses his lips lightly against mine in a chaste kiss, then tucks his nose against the crook of my neck and inhales deeply. His scent, a combination of sea and forest, pervades my senses and I relax against him despite the dire situation we face.

"Why can't I remember the last few days, Little Mir?" He whispers against the skin of my neck.

I shake my head lightly, then reply, "I need you to wait for me to explain later, we don't have time right now. Everyone has been under the effects of a potion, but we aren't safe here to discuss it."

Vlad growls again, his face immediately lifting from my hair to glare at Leif.

I swat at him to catch his attention. "Leif isn't the problem. Please, can you trust me?"

Vlad's amber gaze returns to my face, filled with earnestness. "Of course."

Releasing a relieved breath, I step away from the

comfort of Vlad's arms and repeat the process with the vial. I pour a sip of the potion into the glass, forcing Sylvia, Marc, and Alex to each take a sip.

Instead of waiting beside each one for the potion to take effect, I move quickly, flitting from one person to the next. They all seem to shake off the lingering traces of the apathy potion within seconds of each other.

Before anyone can speak, I hold a single palm in the air. "We aren't safe here and I don't think there's time for a full explanation yet. I need you to trust me, and once we've escaped from Haven, I'll tell you everything."

My friends nod their agreement, and I'm immediately grateful for their trust. I look to Leif, hoping he doesn't screw us over. I'm unsure if he's trustworthy, but I also know we don't have another choice if we want to leave without getting caught by his father.

His muddy brown gaze connects with mine and he nods, wordlessly, like he's encouraging me to ask the question poised on the tip of my tongue. I blurt it out before I lose my nerve, "Leif, can you get us somewhere safe? We need a place to form our next plan."

His gaze leaves mine, and he scans the room. I follow his eyes, taking in the anxious expressions of my friends. The room is so quiet, you could hear a pin drop. After the most torturous minute of my life, Leif's gaze returns to mine and he says, "I know a place. We leave in five."

"Thank you," I whisper, my eyes dropping to the floor as I collect my thoughts.

Turning to my friends, I instruct, "Gather anything from your rooms that you need, as quickly as possible. Then meet back here in four minutes."

Leif shrugs as my friends exit the room to pack their belongings, addressing my earlier statement, "Don't thank me until we've made it out."

The minutes pass quickly and I rush to shove all of my books and a few articles of clothing into a backpack. I scan the rest of my belongings, but nothing else is irreplaceable, so I leave it behind. Standing, I move to the hallway and am quickly joined by the rest of the group.

Leif leads us to the travel tunnel at the far end of the hall. We gather in a small circle to listen to his whispered instructions, "I've thought of somewhere safe for us, but I need you all to drink a sip of this. It's the only way for you to gain access." He removes another thin vial from his pocket, this one containing a vibrant fuchsia liquid.

"What is it?" Sylvia asks, wrinkling her nose like Leif asked her to drink toilet water.

"It's a potion that will allow you entry to a spelled private property. Drink it or the spell at the location will make you physically unable to enter."

"Has your dad drank this?" I ask.

"No. No one but my sister," Leif replies in a somber tone.

Nodding, I snatch the vial from him and take a small sip. The second the liquid hits my tongue, it bubbles and fizzles like carbonated water. Instead of melting away as I swallow, the feeling intensifies, spreading rapidly through my entire mouth. I'm about to panic as the fizzy feeling crawls down my throat, but just as quickly as it began, the sensation dissipates.

Frowning over the sensations, or lack thereof, in my mouth, I pass the vial to the left. Once we've all taken a sip, Leif pockets the potion. "Okay, so you need to think 'Leif's Hidden Lair' as you enter the travel tunnels."

Sylvia snorts and Leif's eyes narrow in response. Before they can't start an argument, we don't have time for, I interject, "Do we need to know anything else?"

Leif declines with a shake of his head, then leaps into the travel tunnel and disappears from sight.

The five of us exchange a glance, then Alex shrugs. He hops into the tunnel with a war cry, following Leif. Marc follows, then Sylvia, leaving Vlad and I standing in the hallway.

"Are we doing the right thing?" I ask, briefly allowing myself to question our sudden alliance with Leif.

"Come here," Vlad murmurs, pulling me into his solid chest. Resting his chin against the top of my head, he says, "I'm sorry for whatever happened recently. I can't remember anything after the first day." I open my mouth to respond, but Vlad continues, "I won't let Leif get close to you again or hurt you again, but we can't stay here."

I nod, relaxing into his firm hold and the moment of peace. It doesn't last longer than a few seconds, though. A menacing shout echoes down the hall, shattering the illusion of safety.

Quickly separating, I glance in the direction of the noise and spot Archibald Golden leading a group of robed witches in our direction. They must have come through a different travel tunnel.

Vlad grabs onto my hand, distracting me. Our gazes connect briefly, then he pulls me into his chest before leaping into the tunnel. I clear my mind, forcing the thought *Leif's Hidden Lair* on repeat, hoping we make it.

7
THE LAIR

Mirabella

The travel tunnel unceremoniously drops us in the middle of nowhere. Leif acts like this is a normal occurrence and leads us through the overgrown woods while humming a cheerful tune. The rest of us trudge along silently, scanning our surroundings. It's clear everyone except the crazy Canadian is on edge.

We finally reach the tree line, which opens up to a clearing, and I feel my eyes widen as my tension slowly ebbs away. Leif continues forward while humming, but my feet root me in place.

Straight ahead of us is an enormous cabin-like structure. It's shaped in an A-frame with a large, rectangular structure sprawling out behind it. The entire front appears to be made of glass, with a brick-red siding covering the rest of the building.

The rest of the group trickles around me, continuing forward as my gaze rakes over the front porch. Two rocking chairs sit on one side, with a porch swing across from it. Leif's "hidden lair" is surprisingly homey. I had expected to land in a damp, gloomy cave with a hidden home somewhere, but this looks like it could easily belong to some grandmotherly type of person who prefers to live in privacy.

Vlad grips onto my hand, intertwining our fingers and dragging me forward to catch up with the rest of our friends. I look over my shoulder and glimpse the pink-topped spires of Haven's castle, just visible over the tops of the trees. They seem so far away a feeling of safety coats me, and I turn back around, forcing my feet to move faster so we can see the inside of the "Lair".

We reach the porch as Leif unlocks the front door, he flings his arm to the side in a dramatic sweep and exclaims, "Welcome to my humble lair, eh."

Ignoring Leif's strange... Leifness, I walk past his arm through the open door and my jaw drops. From outside, the structure provides little indication of the magnificent space contained inside. Immediately upon entering, I step into a room with a twenty-foot ceiling comprised of crisscrossed logs. Against the far wall, a massive stone fireplace is already lit, allowing heat to penetrate the slightly chilly air.

A pair of luxurious, emerald couches sit at an angle near the heat and I slowly wander towards them. The rest of my group filters in behind me and I hear Sylvia gasp at her first glimpse of Leif's admittedly impressive space.

Shedding my backpack, I sink into the couch, leaning heavily against the back. I feel as though I've aged a hundred years in the time since my eighteenth birthday and I'm exhausted down to the marrow of my bones.

The fire helps to soothe some of my tension and rid the slight chill from the fall air. My thoughts wander until someone hovers over me, blocking my sight of the fireplace. Lifting my head, I connect with a muddy gaze and exhale a tired sigh.

"Why don't we use the rest of the day to relax and clean up? We'll be safe here for a few days yet, and it's best to form a plan when we're feeling refreshed, eh?" Leif suggests in a low voice, settling onto the arm of the couch, near my head.

The rest of my friends are scattered about the room, but Leif's eyes never leave mine to acknowledge them. He stares me down, eventually quirking a brow, like my response is the only one that matters. Without much thought, I nod once, easily embracing the idea of avoiding the heavy conversation I know is imminent. At least for one more day.

A smirk edges onto Leif's lips, and he pivots. "Please follow me, Mira Love and friends."

He leads us through the living room into a long hallway of closed doors. Stopping at the closest one, he taps the door. "Wolf boy."

Moving to the opposite side of the hall, he states, "Blondie 1."

The one immediately after receives the next tap. "Blondie 2."

Skipping three doors, he taps another. "Sylvia," he says, offering a small bow and a smile. She grins in return, immediately opening the door and leaving me in the hallway with the guys. I move to the next door, expecting that to be my room for our stay.

Leif stops me with a hand on my elbow. "Ahh, not that one, Mira Love," he states.

He uses his grip to guide me further down the hall, past another four doors. His palm slips down my arm to grab my hand and he intertwines our fingers before stopping at the second to last door in the long hall. "This, Mira Love, is your room."

Leif uses his free hand to push open the door and reveal a massive room beyond. My eyes widen as they skim over the space, catching a small sitting area with another fireplace and two armchairs. Past that is a beautiful four-poster bed with white bedding. The additional furniture is elegant and appears handmade.

I turn to face Leif, my eyes connecting with his. "It looks beautiful Leif, thank you."

His smirk transitions into a full-blown grin, and he squeezes my hand lightly. "I'm glad you approve. I'm right next door if you need anything. Anything at all, at any time."

I open my mouth to respond, when Vlad's rumbling voice interjects, "She won't need anything. At least not from you."

The words, spoken just behind my left ear, burst the bubble that Leif and I's connected palms and gaze created. I startle, releasing my grip and stepping backwards, straight into Vlad's arms. Tipping my head back, I hope to connect with a set of amber eyes, but they're locked in a staring contest with Leif.

Sighing, I step past the two boys and into the bedroom. I have a feeling this macho act of dominance could last a while and I'm ready for a nap. Leaving the door open for Vlad, I slink forward, making a beeline for the extra-large king bed.

I slip under the cover seconds before Vlad enters, gently closing the door behind himself. He deposits my backpack from the living room onto the dresser. My eyes follow his muscular jean and T-shirt clad body as he approaches the bed.

A thrumming of nerves begins low in my belly, as I remember the night Vlad and I had in Hope. It was one of the last times we spent alone together prior to all the craziness within Florence and Haven. A small part of me wonders if Vlad is reliving the same memory. If he is, maybe we'll pick up where we left off.

Vlad interrupts my thoughts by kneeling against the end of the bed. As my eyes skim over his roman nose and plump lips, he grabs onto my ankles underneath the covers and drags me further down the downy, soft mattress.

I release a soft squeal which barely has time to pass my lips before the covers slip over my head. With a giggle, I shove the blankets away and lock with a set of amber orbs. The emotion in Vlad's eyes takes my breath away.

We continue to wordlessly communicate as his lips descend towards mine. My eyes flutter shut seconds before they connect. A soft, breathy sigh escapes as Vlad claims my entire being in that one kiss.

His lips slide against mine, conveying desire coated in layers of affection I'm not ready to name yet. That one kiss washes away all the lonely, terrible feelings I've experienced during the days spent in Haven.

I lose myself to Vlad, arching my chest into his as he settles between my legs, connecting our cores. One of his hands leaves the bed and lightly skims down my side, his fingertips drifting down my ribcage to rest on my hip.

Vlad pulls back, his amber gaze connecting with mine. His eyes fill with a silent question and I nod. Smirking, his fingers drift to the hem of my shirt, which he wordlessly pulls over my head. I fight the urge to cover my plain bra as the fabric clears my head.

He leans in and whispers, "My beautiful Little Mir." Then proceeds to pepper the skin of my neck with soft, open-mouthed kisses. His lips drift down further, connecting with my collarbone, then the skin above the cup of my bra.

I watch the path of his lips and our gazes connect again. Vlad maintains eye contact as his hands slip behind my back and unclasp my bra. Shrugging my shoulders, I help him rid me of the pesky clothing.

The second it's flung off the bed, Vlad's plush lips immediately lock onto my left nipple. He licks and sucks, dragging a deep moan from the pit of my soul as his hand connects with the firm skin of my right breast.

My hands snake underneath Vlad's shirt, my nails scraping against his taut abs as his lips continue their assault. Frantically, I tug at the edge of the fabric, suddenly wanting to be skin to skin. Vlad's lips barely leave mine. He offers a quick smirk and does the work for me, yanking his shirt off one handed before descending on me once more.

His hands flit from my chest to the button on my jeans. Vlad's warm fingers brush against my lower belly as he works to undo the closure. He slides the fabric over my skin and I lift my bottom up to help.

Vlad pauses his kisses as his fingers slide under the edge of my panties. His eyes seek mine once more, the amber orbs wordlessly asking for permission. I nod once, and Vlad tears away the last scrap of clothing separating us.

Feeling emboldened by the heated gaze Vlad skims down my body, my hand finds his hardened length still covered by his jeans. He groans into my mouth, stilling his movements as I try to unbutton his jeans, but my fingers fumble around clumsily, like I've never worked a button before.

Vlad chuckles, a sexy sound that I feel all the way down to the tips of my toes. He pushes my fingers away and takes over, unbuttoning his pants and shimmying them down. His skin barely leaves mine, but I immediately miss his warmth in the seconds it does.

As he settles his burly body between my legs once more, part of my brain tries to protest taking things further. It insists I'm using this, using Vlad, as a distraction from everything else going on. Especially the crazy events that occurred in Haven.

Shoving the thought away, I arch into Vlad as his fingers seek my center. Just before they hit their intended destination, the doorknob to my room jiggles. Thankfully, Vlad clicked the lock, and it doesn't budge.

Unfortunately, the person on the other side doesn't get the hint. A loud banging follows, like someone is hitting their palm against the wood. Soon a voice joins the noise. "Mira, I know you're in there. Come join us in the kitchen, Leif is making dinner and I miss you. I barely remember this past week and I feel like I didn't see you at all," Sylvia whines.

Vlad and I groan simultaneously in frustration.

Clearing my throat, I reply, "Yeah, okay, I'll be out in a sec." I'm hoping my words will be enough to convince Sylvia to leave. If she leaves quickly, Vlad and I can steal a few more kisses, at the very least.

Instead of leaving, Sylvia tacks on, "Have you seen Vlad? He wasn't in his room and no one knows where he is."

Vlad coughs to cover a laugh, then rumbles out, "I'm in here too Sylvia. We'll be out in a few minutes."

"Oh my god," she squeals, her tone a combination of embarrassed excitement. "Err, sorry. I'll see you in a few," she rushes out, then I hear her footsteps pounding against the floor as she scurries away.

My cheeks heat in embarrassment and my arousal deflates as I wonder what Sylvia plans to tell the others. Sighing, I tear my gaze from the door to meet Vlad's. A hank of his inky hair has fallen across his forehead and I reach up, tucking it back against the rest. He nestles into my hand briefly, then pecks my lips.

"We should probably get dressed," he whispers.

"Yeah. If we wait too long, they may break down the door to come get us," I murmur, in an equally quiet tone.

Vlad nods, his muscles rippling as he lifts himself off the bed. I admire his abs, then his toned back as he bends over, scooping our clothes into a pile and placing them on the bed.

His eyes run one more searing glance over my body. Then, with a look of reluctance, he hands me my pile of my clothes.

. . .

THE KITCHEN IS AN EXPANSIVE, open space with dark navy cabinets and white granite countertops that appear to be littered with every possible kitchen gadget. Leif stands in front of a six-burner stove, stirring and flipping pots and pans with unknown contents at random intervals. Although I'm not sure what he's cooking, it smells amazing. My grumbling stomach reminds me I haven't eaten for hours and I suddenly find that I'm ravenous.

Tearing my eyes away from Leif, my eyes connect with Sylvia's expectant gaze. Her expression makes me realize I missed a question.

"Err, can you repeat that?" I ask. "Delicious food smells distracted me."

Sylvia giggles in response, then states, "I could tell. I just asked if you found any information while you were in Haven. I can barely remember being there at all, besides the first day." Her jovial expression falls into a frown with the words.

"About that," I start. Clearing my throat, I increase the volume of my words to include the entire kitchen in the conversation. "I actually need to tell you all something."

I wait until every eye in the room, except for Leif's, focuses on me. Inhaling a deep breath, I blurt, "We ran from Haven because Leif and I discovered you were being spelled by Archibald Golden. It's the reason you can't remember anything from the days we were there. If any memories eventually return, it will also explain your strange behavior. You four were under the effects of an apathy potion."

Vlad and Marc simultaneously release deep rumbly growls and I desperately try to think of words to soothe their agitated wolves.

Surprisingly, it's Leif that comes to my rescue. "It shouldn't have any long-term effects. The potion you drank to clear the apathy potion from your system may have you feeling groggy, but that will pass soon." He turns away from the stove and scans the room, briefly connecting gazes with each of my friends. "I'm sorry for the actions of my father, and that I wasn't able to stop them sooner."

His words appear to placate both of the shifters in the room and the growling ceases.

A flash of purple catches my attention and my eyes seek Sylvia. She's wearing an unreadable expression, but when she notices me looking, she forces a smile to her lips. "Well, thank you for saving us... that explains a lot."

I walk towards the dining room table, where Sylvia is sitting with the twins. Sinking into the seat next to her, I wrap an arm around her back and squeeze her into my side. She returns the half hug and rests her head against my shoulder.

"I'm sure that information was a lot to process," I begin, unsure how to apologize for the feeling of violation I'm confident the apathy potion evoked. "If you need anything, let Leif and I know, especially if you feel any lingering effects," I state, making eye contact with each of my friends while maintaining my hold on Sylvia.

"Thanks Mira," Sylvia whispers.

The sentiment is echoed by Marc and Alex, while Vlad slips into the seat beside me.

"I found something, I'm not sure if it's important," I state. "Do you want me to go grab it or wait to talk until tomorrow?" I ask.

"There's no time like the present," Alex replies, offering me a reassuring smile.

Nodding, I scurry away from the table and down the long hall to my room. Not wanting to keep my friends waiting, I tear open my backpack and snatch the green leather-bound text I stole from the archives.

As I return to the table, I note the awkward silence that's descended upon the room and wonder if it's always like that when I'm not around. Shaking off the thought, I slip back into my seat with the book and glance around, suddenly feeling uncertain about my discovery. "I don't know if this is all that important..."

"What drew you to the book in the first place?" Marc asks in a soft, encouraging tone.

"It just felt important, I can't explain it. The book appears to contain information about shifter legacies and reminded me of a witch legacy book that Leif showed me. Now that I'm saying this out loud, it sounds silly. I don't know how legacies change anything, or why I stole this book from the archives," I respond with a self-deprecating laugh.

Leif clicks off all the burners, rounding the corner into the dining area. He stops directly behind my chair and extends a hand next to my face. "May I?" He asks.

I wordlessly hand it over, and Leif walks to the seat at the head of the table. He flips through the book quickly, stopping on a page about halfway through. His gaze dances across the book and I wonder at what he's found that's so fascinating.

As if he can sense my curiosity, Leif turns the book to face the table and points at a black and white portrait that covers the entire left page. My eyes flit over the image expecting it to be unimportant, but it isn't.

A growl rips free from Vlad and he grits out, "Why the fuck is there a drawing of me in that book?"

8

THE SUGGESTION

Vlad

Confusion and the ever-present anger hum in my blood. The two emotions combine into a surge of adrenaline that makes me want to punch something.

Somehow, a single touch against my thigh from Mira's tiny palm soothes away enough of the urge. I'm able to remain seated at the dining table without incident. She continues to rub gentle circles on my jean-clad skin and my thoughts clear.

After a minute or two, I feel like I'll be able to interact with Mira and the ragtag collection of her friends in a semi-normal manner. I tune into the mundane conversation occurring around me. They've given me some time to collect myself, waiting to pursue the legacy conversation until after dinner, so I haven't missed anything important.

"What is all this food you cooked, Leif?" I hear Mira ask.

The stupid prick smiles warmly at my girlfriend as I reach for my glass of water. I applaud myself as I take a sip instead of throwing it at his head. Small victories.

He scans the table and points to each dish, as he names them, "Grilled pineapple chicken, glazed asparagus, quinoa salad, and that over there is a regular salad with a raspberry vinaigrette."

"Whoa, you were able to throw this all together so quickly. I'm impressed," Mira replies, with a gentle smile, as her palm continues to trace designs on my leg.

"Why such an eclectic mix?" I grit out.

Leif shrugs, his eyes never leaving Mira as she scoops quinoa or some shit onto her plate. "It's just what was in the cupboards..." he trails off, then adds, "I wasn't expecting to come here this week, so there is an odd mix of food leftover from my last visit."

I nod in response, accepting the dish Mira passes me. Before I place any food on my plate, I cautiously sniff the contents, not even caring if I'm being obvious. I don't trust this Leif dude after the crap he pulled the last time he was around.

To be honest, I'm not sure how he became involved in our little adventure. He's already proven his father heavily influences his actions and everyone in the Golden clan is all sorts of fucked up. The last thing we need is to invite saboteurs into our midst. It's something I'll need to speak with Mira about after we finish eating.

A chuckle from across the table has my eyes leaving the dish my nose is in, to meet a pair of shit brown eyes. Leif smirks, aiming the sardonic expression in my direction, and I barely cage the growl that bubbles up my throat in response.

"Can I help you," I ask, instead.

Leif declines with a shake of his head, his attention drifting to Mira once more, before landing on his plate.

Smug prick.

Mira's fingers dig into my thigh a little deeper, capturing my attention. I glance down at her and see she's eating with her right hand, while her left dances across my leg. I tug her palm into mine, intertwining our fingers and picking up my fork with my other hand.

Shoving aside thoughts of Leif and his questionable motives, I dig into the meal he prepared for us. I almost wish it was disgusting, just to have a significant flaw in the dude that I could pick on besides the fact that he's in love with my girl.

Unfortunately, the food is edible. Borderline delicious, if I were willing to admit such a thing about someone I hate.

My stomach is like an empty cavern and even after a second helping, it's still rumbling for more. I scan the table and realize everyone else has stopped eating. I restrain myself from heaping even more food onto my plate.

Now that we're done, we can discuss the book which is more important than the bottomless pit of my stomach.

Leif walks around the table collecting plates and piling them into the sink. He doesn't immediately return, but rather pauses to press a few buttons on a fancy looking coffee pot which instantly steams and hisses under his commands.

He leans against the counter, patiently waiting as if we have all the time in the world for the appliance to do... whatever it's doing. As if she can sense my irritation, Mira gently squeezes my palm and mutters, "It'll be okay. In just a few minutes, we'll figure this out together."

I return the squeeze in silent appreciation. I'm impatient to see the book Leif tucked away under his chair and nothing Mira says can change that, but I love how thoughtful she is and I want her to know that.

Leif clattering in the kitchen recaptures my attention and my ire peaks as I watch him prepare a tray of tiny mugs filled with espresso and other fixings. When he finally approaches the table, he asks, "Espresso anyone?"

Apparently, I'm the only one that finds Leif to be

the human equivalent of a gnat because the rest of our group readily agrees and Leif stops by every seat to disperse the coffee. Once he's finished, he returns to his seat, and I steeple my hands on the table, ready for the conversation to begin.

I meet a pair of eyes the color of murky, mosquito infested water. "What does the page across from the drawing say?"

Leif smirks, snagging the book from under his seat and returning it to the table. "Hmm let's look," he replies. His freaky long fingers flip through the pages at an excruciatingly slow pace and I'm seconds away from snatching the book from his grasp when he murmurs, "Aha."

He silently skims the page for a moment, then looks at the group. He makes eye contact with everyone else, eyes probing into their souls before finally turning to me. "It appears this book speaks of your lineage," Leif states, sounding far too superior when speaking to someone that shifts into an animal with canines as large as his palms.

My fist clenches in my lap with nails scraping skin as I temper my anger. Mira chimes in before I act on my impulses, "How do you know?"

"Besides the uncanny likeness depicted within its pages?" He retorts.

"Are there any answers in that book or are you wasting our time?" I scoff at Leif.

Instead of answering, he changes the topic. "When

I was in Florence, training Mira Love for her witching exam, I learned that your parents were witches... yet you, clearly, are not. Obviously one witch plus another witch cannot equal a shifter. You had to come from somewhere else, Vlad," Leif states slowly like he's teaching a six-year-old basic math.

I growl low in my throat and Mira resumes her soothing palm circles. Although appreciated, they're no longer doing much to keep me calm in face of the infuriating dick still smirking at me from across the table.

The dick in question merely shrugs and chuckles in response to the sound. "There's no reason to believe you are not a shifter legacy. I don't think you're that special, but we need to find someone who has an archive on shifter lineage and see if we can trace the legacy lines to confirm or not. If we can do that, we'd have a better idea of whether this image reflects your heritage. Obviously, we can't tell by name alone at this point."

"If what you're saying is true, and we need to find out more about Vlad's birth parents... what do we do next?" Mira asks, voicing one of the many questions floating through my mind. Her words are kinder and more eloquent than I'm capable of at this point, and I squeeze her palm lightly in silent gratitude.

"Even if we find out Vlad's birth name, how do we know it will help with the cure? No offense on your gut feeling," Sylvia says, offering my girl a gentle smile.

Mira nods thoughtfully. "None taken."

Alex speaks next, "If we find a way to trace the lineage, maybe we can figure out what happened to the legacies on both sides and find more answers from them. At this point we don't even know what caused the curse. We need to know that before we can help the witches or the shifters."

At the end of his statement, five brows furrow and the room falls into absolute silence. We have a colossal problem, dozens of questions, and no idea where to start. With every step forward, we seem to unearth more secrets and more problems.

Marc is the first to look away from the table. He meets my eyes and suggests, "We should go to our family's ancestral home. Our parents have an expansive collection of witching and shifter history books. They'll be willing to help us and maybe even provide answers."

His eyes leave mine to connect with his twins. They stare at each other for a few seconds and Alex nods. He faces Mira and simply states, "Mira." Then, as if he suddenly remembers there are other people in the room, his gaze flits around the table, "Vlad, Sylva, Leif, it's time for you to meet the Sieves. We need to head to Connecticut."

Silence descends over the table once more as everyone absorbs his words, then Sylvia, Leif, and Mira all speak at once.

"How will they—"

"When should we—"

"I think we should—"

Groaning, I shove away from the table. Marc's knowing gaze meets mine. They flash a small amount of the irritation I'm currently experiencing, as he rises to his feet as well.

Marc trails a few steps behind me as I stride to the door and silence descends in the kitchen. Before I'm able to tug open the door leading outside, Leif's annoyingly accented voice breaks through my consciousness. "Stay within a two-mile radius of the cabin. That's as far as the barrier extends."

I grunt in response, then step through the door without a backwards glance.

Marc shuts the door gently behind us. The click of the latch combined with my first breath of fresh, wilderness air releases a portion of the tension that has built in my chest and shoulders, but not much.

Either the stress from our current situation, or the aftereffects of the apathy potion, has left me with a pounding migraine and the urge to pummel Leif Golden. To be fair, the second is most likely a side-effect of his terrible personality, but a run should cure both issues. At least temporarily.

Marc interrupts my thoughts with a few soft-spoken words. "You okay, man?"

Huffing out a breath, I nod. "Need to run. You in?"

He yanks his shirt off one-handed in response.

Nodding again, I follow suit, quickly shedding my clothes, then allowing the shift to take over.

An undulating wave of pain and transformation consumes me. My body crackles and snaps, breaking and mending every bone in my body as my entire anatomy rearranges itself to accommodate my second form. The shift lasts less than a minute, and the sharp pain subsides seconds after.

I slowly adjust to the new color spectrum. From the corner of my eye, I spot Marc stretching out his muscles to prepare for our night. Raising my snout to the air, I release a long howl, then we leap off the porch and into the trees.

Hours later, Marc and I return to Leif's stupid little hidey hole. All the cabin lights appear to be off, except the porch light, which is casting a small circle of light on the front of the house. The sweet gesture directs my thoughts to Mira and I'm instantly eager to join her in bed.

We redress silently on the front porch. A light ache covers my entire body from the punishing run this evening. Before heading inside, I roll my shoulders back and raise my arms above my head, stretching my taut muscles, I grunt as my shoulder pops, then turn to Marc.

At his nod, we enter the house together. I pause

and lock the door, despite the desolate area and barrier spell, wanting to make sure we're safe after the string of bad luck we've encountered recently.

Without further delay, I hurry to the hall with the bedrooms, quickly bypassing Marc in my rush. I throw a small wave over my shoulder as I pass, not stopping until I hit the door to Mira's room. Testing the handle gently, I find the door unlocked and slip inside.

She's left the bedside lamp turned on, the soft glow illuminating a lump of blankets and a swath of blonde hair floating across the pillows. Mira is barely distinguishable under the covers, and the sight has a pang of... something striking my chest as I listen to her soft breaths for a few seconds.

The pang of... something tries to morph into guilt or regret. This is one of the first moments of peace Mira seems to have had in months and all the problems she's involved in tie back to me. If we had never rekindled our friendship, Mira would never have become involved in shifter business.

Shaking my head, I clear my thoughts before they're able to reignite the rage I left behind in the woods.

Instead of focusing on the past, I yank off my shirt and slip under the covers next to Mira. Despite my attempts to not wake her, the mattress dips under my weight and she rolls into me. Her eyes fly open in panic, relaxing the second she registers who it is that joined her.

"Vlad," she sighs, immediately nestling closer.

"Sorry to wake you," I whisper, then add, "I've missed you."

"I missed you too," she murmurs as sleep reclaims her.

Tilting my face forward, I lay a soft kiss on her forehead, then rest my nose against her hair. Her light, floral scent invades my senses with each inhale and I feel my body relax against the mattress.

Mira releases a contented sigh and nestles closer, her breathing deep and steady. I assume she's asleep, but she murmurs, "We'll find answers, Vlad. To all the questions. We'll figure out if you're a legacy and what that means. And if your parents are out there, we can find them too. I promise I'll help in any way I can."

That pang of... something hits my chest again, but I'm not ready to examine the feeling yet. Instead, I whisper, "Thank you."

She nods gently against me, squeezing her body impossibly closer to mine. "We're in this together."

I kiss her forehead again and listen as she falls back into a deep slumber.

As much as I want to welcome sleep, it evades me. My arms grip Mira tightly, cradling her to my chest like precious cargo while my brain tries to solve problems without enough facts and information. I've always known I was adopted, but now I may be some shifter legacy.

Why wouldn't my family want me? If being a legacy

is important, they should've protected me and kept me. Right?

Questions continue to circle around my brain, making both my human and wolf halves feel entirely unsettled. Eventually I wear myself out and fall into a restless sleep.

9

THE ALLY

Mirabella

I wake slowly, lightly stretching and arching into the warm form molded against my back. Vlad's ocean-pine scent has permeated every corner of the room, alerting me of his presence without catching sight of his face.

He mumbles something unintelligible, tightening his grip as I attempt to escape. I wriggle around in his arms, laying a soft, chaste kiss against his lips. Then, I shove at his chest.

With a loud grumble, Vlad releases me. I clamber off the bed, giggling at his ill-humored grunt, as I head to the bathroom. Somehow, in the span of one summer, I've become accustomed to waking up with Vlad in my bed more often than not. During this time, I've learned he is not a morning person.

My stomach grumbles loudly as I step back into my room from the en-suite and the sound determines my next activity. Instead of climbing back into the warm bed with the hunky guy still sleeping there, I exit into the hall.

Almost immediately, I slam into a hard body, barely catching myself against the doorframe before hitting the floor. I glance up to spot a tall form with blonde hair hovering just outside my door.

"Oh, Leif, hi," I stammer out.

"Good morning, Mira Love," he says with a slight smirk. "I was just coming to wake you. I am about to start breakfast and wanted to know if you had any preferences?"

"I'm starving, but I can eat cereal or whatever you have that's easy... you don't need to cook anything."

Leif waves off my words and turns on his heel. He strides down the hallway, rounding the corner out of sight before my brain catches up with the fact that he's left. I trail after him, stopping at the island lined with stools, observing as he pulls out various items from the fridge.

"We have sausage, bacon, eggs, or I can make pancakes. What is your preference?"

Realizing there's no way to derail this train, I shrug and hoist myself onto one of the barstools, using the counter and bottom rung to make up for my severe lack of height. "Uhm, chef's choice," I finally say.

Leif's muddy gaze connects with mine across the

kitchen. He scans my expression, eyes flitting over my face, then briefly down my body. He wordlessly turns away and I release the breath I was holding for unknown reasons.

Silence stretches, creating a strange tension in the kitchen as bacon sizzles and pops on the stove. I compare the experience to eating in Vlad's house for some reason. Maybe because it's the only other experience I have with a guy cooking me breakfast.

Thinking of breakfast with Vlad immediately leads me to thoughts of his parents, then mine. My torso sinks to rest against the cool, marble counter of the island as I remember my favorite parts of Florence and wrestle with the idea that I may never be able to return. The line of thought makes my heart ache and my appetite peters.

I'm tempted to return to bed, to Vlad's warm arms, but before I'm able to drag my body out of the barstool, a commotion sounds in the hallway. Doors slam, punctuated by shouting. Seconds later, footsteps pound across the hardwood floor. The sounds approach the kitchen and my pulse speeds up in reaction. My body transitions to high alert and I descend from my stool and twirl to face the living room, preparing to face the oncoming threat.

I pace a step closer towards the noise, intent on answers, but I'm shoved behind Leif's lanky form. Just past his shoulder, I spot the spatula he was using to flip eggs held in front of him like he's wielding a weapon.

Marc, Alex, and Sylvia round the corner, laughing and shoving each other as they bound across the floor. Upon seeing them, Leif's shoulders instantly relax and he drops the spatula, returning to the stove with an exasperated shake of his head.

I remain rooted in place, watching in horror as my friends act half their age. My heart drops closer to the floor with each shove and shriek.

Are they under the effects of the apathy potion again? Did Leif's cure not work?

Alex pushes against Marc, shoving him into the living room and causing him to lose his balance. With his brother out of the way, he dives onto the floor, sliding across the hardwood like he's a seal with the fingers of his left hand outstretched in front of his body. His momentum ceases a half a foot away, and he taps his fingertips against the tips of my toes. "Winner."

Sylvia and Marc enter the kitchen seconds after and they groan simultaneously. "You cheated," Sylvia accuses, slipping into the stool I recently vacated. Her furrowed brow turns into a smile as our eyes connect, "Hey, Mir. And Leif."

"You're just a sore loser," Alex admonishes addressing Sylvia's earlier statement as he rises slowly to his feet to stand in front of me. I crane my neck back slightly, meeting his green gaze. He steps closer, causing my neck to tilt back even further, then he wraps his arms around my shoulders, resting his chin lightly atop my head.

The action startles, but I quickly return the grip, placing my hands around his waist. "Is everything okay?" I ask as his grip tightens, smooshing my face against his chest.

Alex sighs, then mutters, "Yeah. I just missed you. It feels like we've barely seen each other recently and I wanted to apologize for not being around when you needed me."

I relax fully into his grip, rubbing my palm against his back in a soothing motion. His words ease my fears that the apathy potion effects were still lingering, but I struggle to voice my thoughts. "Thank you for your apology. Being in Haven was kind of terrible, but it wasn't your fault. I'm just glad we're all together again now."

Alex nods, his chin tapping against the top of my head before he takes a step back. His emerald eyes connect with mine briefly. He steps away and joins Sylvia at the island, easily sliding into a bar stool.

I'm shocked when Marc approaches me next. He offers a slightly shy smile, then softly asks, "May I?"

I know Marc, the real Marc, least. Despite his confession that he watched over me since arriving in Florence and saved me from the deranged wolf at the expo, our relationship is still tentatively blossoming.

Nodding, I step forward, allowing him to wrap his arms around me in a mimic of the moment I just experienced with his brother. Unlike my moment with Alex, his arms and body are stiff, held a few inches away as if he's worried he might make me uncomfortable. I pat his back in a sisterly manner. "I'm glad you're back to normal too," I state quietly.

I feel Marc nod. "I've spent too much time being influenced by outside sources recently."

His words process slowly, and I recall his experience being lost to his wolf. Days after he returned to his human form, he was spelled, causing him to act differently than he normally would. I open my mouth to offer words of comfort, but Leif interrupts me with a scoff. "Are you going to spend your entire morning hugging in the center of the kitchen, Mira Love?"

AFTER BREAKFAST our group agrees to take the rest of the day off, to recuperate. We all need time to embrace our new normal, think over the discoveries we made last night, and regroup. A day won't make a huge difference in anything but our mental health and tomorrow we can go back to saving the world. Or at least the shifters.

Vlad and I retreat to the couch, lounging against one another in silence as the rest of the group disperses throughout the "Lair". We enjoy the semblance of privacy and I nestle against his chest, allowing a languid feeling to take over as I embrace our day of peace.

Silence reigns and I find my eyes drifting shut. The moment of stillness has my body wanting to catch up on much-needed rest. Vlad lays a palm against my arm, his fingers lightly dancing across my skin. The simple movement combined with exhaustion quickly lulls me to sleep.

Sometime later, Vlad wakes me by lightly skimming a hand across the surface of my arm accompanied by a question. "Are you feeling okay, Little Mir?"

I sigh, nuzzling my head into his chest, contemplating possible answers prior to responding. "So much has happened recently," I finally say. Vlad continues sweeping his fingers across my skin silently. It's as if he knows I need a few minutes to organize the words swirling about in my mind.

When I open my mouth again, I blurt, "It feels like this is never going to end. With every answer we think we find, we unearth a million more questions. What will happen if we can't help the shifters?" I hesitate briefly, then add, "When I confronted Archibald Golden, he said the only way for witches to break their curse was for all the wolves to lose their humanity."

Vlad's hand stops moving the second my words sink in. He places his fingers underneath my chin and tilts my head back so our eyes can connect. His amber gaze scans my face and it looks like he's searching for answers, but I don't have any more to provide.

"Did you already tell this to the others?" He asks.

I shake my head without breaking eye contact. "I

haven't had a chance yet. Dinner dissolved pretty quickly last night. Then, today, we all needed the chance... to be normal. I was planning to bring it up tomorrow."

"I don't know if this can wait," Vlad replies, his voice rumbling with each syllable. "We may be in more danger than we originally thought. If the witches have knowledge about the curse and are actively preventing a cure, they're likely hunting us down as we speak."

He sits upright, dragging me with him, but I barely notice. I'm too startled by his astute conclusion. Why hadn't I thought of that already?

Coven Leader Golden fully admitted to my witches exams being sabotaged. If my Coven was willing to stoop that low, is there anything they wouldn't do in order to stop us?

Vlad helps me to my feet, as the urgency of our situation becomes apparent. Before we're able to move from the living room to gather our friends, the door to the cabin opens with a bang. The wood hits the wall stationed behind the door, revealing a lanky girl with flowing blonde hair standing in the doorframe.

A growl erupts from Vlad's chest besides me. The rumbling sound tears from his throat and fills the room. It isn't directed at me, yet the hairs on my arms stand on end in awareness anyway.

His growl is absolutely menacing.

The blonde hesitates briefly, but steps forward all the same. The action has me attempting to move in her direction, around the barrier of Vlad's body. I want to meet her, since she's either brave or stupid enough to ignore the warning issued by the furious shifter in the room.

"I need Leif, now. Where is he?" The blonde demands, wisely stopping just past the door.

I place my hand against Vlad's chest to calm him in the only way I know how. Addressing the unknown female, I ask, "Who are you?"

Her features look familiar, but I can't immediately place where I've seen her before.

"I'm Leif's sister," she replies. She strides further into the room, perching on the edge of an armchair and crossing her arms. It's a bold move considering it places her less than two feet away from my angry wolf. "We don't really have time for a full-on interrogation. Just tell me where he is."

The second she states who she is, I spot their similarities in her thin lips, brown eyes and long limbs. Then I remember seeing her when we first arrived in Haven.

As if summoned, Leif jogs in through the front door. His eyes instantly seek me out. Relief is apparent in his gaze as his eyes land on my body standing near Vlad's side. He runs an assessing glance down my form without once acknowledging the man next to me.

The rest of our group appears in the doorway behind him and he nods once in my direction before turning his attention to his sister. "Annika, what are you doing here?"

She frowns, then quickly neutralizes her expression. "Father is on his way. He's been attacking your barrier all morning. I just found out he's broken through. I have a small head start, barely any at all. You need to leave right now, if you want to make it out before he breaks down the front door."

Her words spring our group into action. My friends rush down the hall, already aware of what needs to be done. We've had two recent situations where we've had to pack our belongings quickly, after all.

Vlad urges me to accompany him down the hall to the bedrooms, but I decline with a shake of my head. A brief assessing look and a nod later, he makes a beeline to the hall, murmuring, "I'll grab your bag."

Knowing Vlad is gathering my belongings, I allow my gaze to return to Annika. "Why did you come here? Why help us?" I ask, wanting to believe in her, but too suspicious of her motives, purely based on her last name.

Annika stands, uncrossing her arms as she rises. She walks to the door and I think she plans to leave without answering. She shocks me when she stops in the entryway, twisting her head and seeking my eyes with her familiar muddy brown gaze.

The look is probing, searching for something unknown. Apparently, she finds the answer she's looking for because she speaks in a tone so low I'm force to lean forward to hear. "I have my own reasons for wanting to help the shifters." Her eyes drift to Leif before returning to my face. "Maybe someday we'll have time to talk about it, Mira."

She doesn't give me the chance to ask more, striding out of the cabin seconds after the words leave her lips. I step forward, tempted to chase after her. Vlad reappears in the living room, stopping me in my tracks as he holds out both our backpacks.

"Do we need to go back to the travel tunnels?" He asks, aiming his question in Leif's direction.

Leif shakes his head and strides across the living room and into the kitchen. He opens a door on the far side of the island, across from the stove. I had previously assumed it led to a pantry, but once opened it reveals a compact room containing an empty door frame and nothing else.

"Is this another portal?" I ask in awe, stopping just outside the door.

Marc, Alex, and Sylvia appear nearby as Leif nods. "Yes, but no more questions for now. If my sister came here to warn us, time is of the essence. She wouldn't get involved otherwise. Now, everyone in and close the door behind you."

He pulls a vial from his pocket and dumps it on the floor directly below the portal as he issues instructions. He shouts a few words that sound like they're in another language. As the door to the room shuts with a quiet click, the liquid climbs up the sides of the portal's frame, filling it with a shimmery, silver gas.

Leif motions us forward, and my group crowds around the portal. Instead of joining us, Leif walks back to the door leading out to the kitchen. I track his movements with my eyes, watching as he snags a backpack I hadn't previously noticed off the handle. He removes a vial from the bag, then places the straps over his shoulders.

He throws the vial against the only exit, and I wince as glass shatters everywhere. By the time my eyes reopen fully, half the door has disappeared. It's as if the potion is eating away at the wood, forming a solid wall in its place.

When Leif rejoins us, the door is entirely gone, leaving us enclosed in a room with no exits. Besides the portal.

"We are headed to Connecticut to meet the Sieves. The portal will transport you directly there..." Leif states, pausing as if he wants to say more. He shakes his head, then adds, "See you soon."

With those parting words, he walks through the empty doorframe, into the silvery shimmer and out of sight. Vlad grabs my hand and drags me through, with the twins and Sylvia on our heels. Right before we blink out of sight, a commotion sounds in the kitchen, on the other side of the wall. A gasp leaves my body as we zip through time and space.

We barely made it without getting caught. I

suppress a shudder as I think about what would have happened to us if Annika hadn't shown up.

My gratitude for Leif's sister quickly flees as I land in a heap on a large, grassy lawn. Although less unexpected than before, our group sprawls just as ungracefully as the first time we used a portal. Thankfully, I land on the twins and not the other way around. I'm unsure if I would survive under their combined weight.

Rising to my feet, I turn my head to the side and spot Leif standing off to the side. His eyes are surveying my crew with his lips turned up in a smirk. He wordlessly watches us untangle our limbs from one another.

"How did you land on your feet?" I ask, incredulous.

Leif chuckles, "Maybe someday I'll show you, Mira Love."

I open my mouth to respond when a tawny-colored wolf the size of a small sedan runs by our group, interrupting our conversation. His footsteps slow, and he sniffs in my direction before continuing onto the porch of the house. My eyes track his movements and I notice a willowy blonde woman is already standing ahead of us, observing the pile of adults in her yard.

My gaze widens as I take in the home behind her. It's a white colonial, expanding far into the distance on either side of the columned porch. The flat front is peppered with at least twenty shuttered windows, giving a small indication of the amount of space inside.

Snapping and cracking noises sound from the porch, capturing my attention. I tear my eyes away from the home in time to see a naked man rise to his feet on the wooden deck. Thankfully shrubbery and a railing cover the important bits and he pulls on a robe before leaving the privacy they offer. Once clothed, he joins the woman standing in full view just outside the front door.

"Marc, Alex, is that you?" She calls, as she wraps an arm around the man beside her.

"Yeah mom," Alex replies. "We have some friends with us... from Florence. We need a place to stay for a while."

She eyes our group, then nods slowly. "All right. I have a potion brewing in my cauldron. The lot of you come in when you're ready. Your father can set you up in the guest house."

Without waiting for a response, she turns on her heel and retreats into the colonial style home. Her husband waves briefly before following her in, probably eager to get dressed before greeting his unexpected guests.

Not wanting to be overheard, Sylvia catches my eye and mouths, "Cauldron?"

I shrug, my eyes equally as wide and surprised as hers. Maybe there's more to the Sieves family than we previously realized.

10

THE SIEVES

Mirabella

Mr. Sieves escorts us through the main house at a quick clip after a brief greeting and handshake. Richard Sieves is an older version of the twins. He's essentially the same height and build, but his hair is a rich, tawny brown with streaks of gray on either side of his temple. The other notable difference between Mr. Sieves and his sons are his pale, green eyes. The light, sea glass color is a stark contrast to the vibrant emerald gaze of his sons.

Between my wandering thoughts and our rapid pace, I barely get a chance to see much of anything during our walk through the main house. I note soft blue walls peppered with scenic paintings in the seconds before we exit through a set of double French doors into an expansive yard.

My steps falter at the impressive sight. A large, sweeping patio extends from the house in the shape of a comma. Just past the edge of cement sits an Olympic sized pool and an in ground hot tub. To their left is a row of low hedges forming an intricate pattern around a small fountain.

I drag my eyes away from the shrubbery, only to catch sight of another house. It's nestled behind a few trees on the far side of the pool. Although it boasts the same white siding as the main home, it appears to be a more modest space.

"Is that the guest house?" I whisper as I step closer. I'm in utter awe of the Sieves home from the small slices I've seen. I can't even imagine why Marc would leave this place and move to our small town in Florence.

Mr. Sieves chuckles, the joyful rumbling snapping me back to the present. "Yes, it is."

"Wow," I mutter, causing another chuckle.

Our group follows Mr. Sieves as he continues moving, winding around the pool. Within a few seconds we're ascending the front steps to stop on a deep-set porch, equipped with a swing. Up close, the building is larger than it looked previously.

Mr. Sieves hands a key from his pocket to Alex, then glances at both of his sons. "Are you planning to stay out here?"

The twins nod in sync, then smile almost simultaneously. Their father grins back, placing a hand in each of their hair, ruffling it lightly. I stifle a giggle as the two twenty somethings both grimace and dodge out of the way of their dad with a groan.

"Okay kiddos, you two know where everything is. If you need anything else, come grab us. Take the night to settle in and we'll sit down for a big breakfast in the morning to get to know each other better." With those parting words, he glances around the group and offers a small wave. "Goodbye everyone, see you tomorrow."

My eyes trail Mr. Sieves as he lopes back across the lawn and into the main house. A small smile crests my face as I watch him leave. I'm glad Marc and Alex suggested we come here, not only for the world class accommodations but also for the chance to meet their family.

The twins clearly inherited their father's easy-going manner. Tomorrow morning, I'll get to know more about their mom, both of their parent's actually, and I'm excited.

Twisting back to face the guest house, I skip inside on the twin's trail, snagging Vlad's hand as I pass him. The interior of the house is sparsely decorated with simple, comfy looking furniture. There is a lack of personal items, which I guess makes sense because it isn't a part of the actual home.

I was expecting the Sieves to offer a pull-out couch and maybe some air mattresses. A tour of the guest space reveals six spacious bedrooms split between the upper and lower levels. Marc stops at the bottom of a staircase, watching as the rest of our group filters into the space nearby. "Alex and I have rooms down here. The rest of the bedrooms are up for grabs."

"We'll share," Vlad whispers into my ear, squeezing my palm to punctuate the sentiment.

I ignore the rush of heat that floods my lower belly at the idea of sharing a bed with Vlad, again. Instead I add, "It's nice of your parents to let us stay here so unexpectedly. Thank you for suggesting it." My gaze connects with Marc's eyes, then Alex's. "Really, this is above and beyond what I expected. Is there anything we can do in return?"

Marc smiles at my offer. "Nah, we'll just eat a few meals with my parents during our stay."

"Our parents love company. They don't get too many visitors... I'm sure they're just happy to have people over. Especially people they can embarrass us in front of," Alex tacks on, sounding sincere.

The group collectively releases a chuckle at his joke. Being here, in the Sieves guesthouse and laughing over silly jokes releases some of the tension that's been building since Annika issued her warning.

Silence reigns for several seconds as we all relax into the comfort of feeling safe. At least for now.

The somber mood is broken by Sylvia, who is staring out the front door longingly. "Does your mom have any spare swimsuits? I can NOT wait to get in that pool!"

Leif straightens from his lounging position against the wall, his eyes alight with interest for the first time since we stepped inside the guest house. "Pool Party, anyone?"

"We have spare swimsuits," Marc states with a shrug, apparently agreeing with Leif's idea.

"No way! Let's change and get into that pool ASAP. We can have a cannonball contest," Sylvia squeals. She hops up and down, clapping her hands together.

Five sets of eyes turn to me expectantly, like I'm the decision maker for our crew. Unsure when this happened, I shrug. "Yeah, we could use a break from all the insanity."

"Follow me," Marc says, wandering toward the back of the main floor, past the staircase.

Sylvia practically floats behind him on her tiptoes, her enthusiasm apparent in each step. I follow at a slower pace, examining more of the house. Though the furnishings and décor are sparse, they are all well-made. The Sieves have good taste.

I'm pulled from my thoughts when Marc abruptly stops, halting our entire chain. He pulls open the last door in the hall, near a side exit. Past the doorframe is a large dresser, a rack filled with colorful pool towels, a full-length mirror, and a settee. Tucked in the back, right corner is a curtained off area, which I guess is for changing.

Marc enters the room, heading straight towards the dresser. He opens one of the bottom two drawers and snags a few different sets of swim trunks without checking the sizes. After he shuts the drawer, he turns to face Sylvia and I as we linger near the door.

"The top two drawers have women's swim tops, the next two have bottoms." He walks away from the dresser and opens a plain white door which leads into a small closet. "We have cover-ups and a few one-pieces in here. Feel free to use whatever you'd like."

He grins at me as my wide eyes scan the room. "This is amazing," I whisper. "Do your parents have a lot of guests over to swim?"

Marc steps closer, his warm emerald eyes searing into mine. "Not too often, but they like to be prepared. Whichever swimsuit you choose is yours to keep. It would be weird to reuse them."

He walks another step closer and I'm forced to tilt my head back to maintain eye contact. Marc's brow furrows, and he opens his mouth, as if to speak. Before he utters a word, he snaps it back shut.

I wait, wondering what thoughts are running through his mind. We still don't know each other well enough for me to tell, but his expression is more serious than usual.

His features finally return to a friendly grin and he squeezes the top of my shoulder gently. "I'll see you out there." Marc walks out the door, tugging it shut behind him as my forehead scrunches in confusion.

"Whoo, thought that boy was going to confess his love for you. That would've been an awkward conversation to observe," Sylvia states.

My eyes snap to her across the room. I was so caught up by Marc; I forgot she was there. She's already digging through the top drawer of the dresser, creating two piles of swim tops. Even from across the room, I can see the dresser is so full the drawers are practically overflowing.

"I doubt that was what he was going to say," I scoff. "It probably had something to do with the shifter curse. Like the reason we are all here." I step closer to Sylvia and redirect the conversation. "Is there anything good in there?"

"Everything. Everything in here is gorgeous." She slams the drawer shut and turns to me, her hands full of different swimsuit pieces. "These five are for you! Go try them on." As I accept the pile she squeals, "I can't wait to get in the water."

Walking away with a grin, I enclose myself in the changing area. There's a small stool inside and I use it to hold the swimsuits as I untangle the strings. Once they're separated, I peek my head around the curtain to find Sylvia in a rainbow-colored string-bikini. The vibrant colors work perfectly with her violet hair, and I grin. "That looks fantastic."

"Thanks, which one did you try on first?" She asks, dragging her gaze away from the mirror.

"Err, do they have anything that isn't so tiny?" I ask in response.

Sylvia places her hands on her hips. "Mira Love. There is no way I'm letting you out of this room in anything but a skimpy bikini. Don't even try."

Sighing, I return to the dressing room and compare the pieces to find the largest one in the bunch. I'm surprised the Sieves offer such scandalous swimwear, but knowing Sylvia, she picked the smallest ones in the entire drawer.

Eventually I shed my clothes and pull on a pale blue top and matching bottoms. The suit consists of four small triangles essentially, but covers slightly more skin than the others with a ruffled edge.

Inhaling deeply, I push the curtain aside to find Sylvia expectantly waiting. "Oh. My. Gosh. Vlad is going to die," she squeals.

"Are you sure I can't wear a one-piece?" I ask, stepping closer to the mirror. I twist side to side, examining the tiny bottoms that feel as if they barely cover my butt.

"No way. All those guys will lose it when they see you. Vlad especially," Sylvia states, then cackles maniacally. "I can't wait."

I release a resigned sigh, then move to the closet. I pluck a semi-sheer robe from a hanger inside. Wrapping it tightly to cover the barely there swimsuit, I turn to Sylvia. "Before we head out, will you braid my hair, so it doesn't tangle?"

. . .

THE GUYS ARE ALREADY OUTSIDE in the pool by the time Sylvia and I have changed and styled our hair. I tug my robe tighter as four sets of eyes watch our descent from the porch and into the backyard. Sylvia sashays down beside me, wearing only her skimpy swimsuit, not caring about the attention aimed in our direction.

The second she reaches the edge of the pool, she screams, "Cannonball." Sylvia jumps into the air, wrapping both of her arms around her legs as she flies into the water. Her landing creates a massive wave of water, dousing the guys and the cement border of the pool.

Her antics successfully divert most of the attention away from me. Marc and Alex use their arms to create waves of water, splashing her over and over as soon as her head surfaces. In a surprise twist, Leif releases a battle cry. He joins team Sylvia, pushing waves of water back at the twins.

I beeline towards a lounge chair, intent on reading the witching text I brought from inside the house. The second my butt hits the plastic surface of the chair, a shadow looms over me. Glancing up, I find Vlad hovering at the end closest to the pool.

"Do I get to see your swimsuit, Little Mir?" He rumbles, pinning me with a heated stare.

Despite my earlier protests, I'm suddenly grateful for Sylvia's swimsuit choice. Smirking lightly, I unfasten the tie to the robe. I slowly slide the fabric open, enjoying the way Vlad's eyes skim down the surface of my skin.

He leans forward, bracing his forearms on the armrests of the chair. "You look amazing. But I think the swimsuit would look better on the floor." Vlad offers a wolfish grin before sealing his lips to mine.

I arch up in the chair, wrapping my arms around his neck and melding my skin to his. Vlad groans as he nips at my bottom lip then devours my mouth. Everything else fades away except for him.

At least it does until we're doused with a stream of cool water. I separate from Vlad with a gasp, swiping the water away from my eyes, then turning to find the source of the interruption. Sylvia stands to the side of the chair with Leif, each of them holding a bucket of water.

Vlad growls low in his throat and lunges, but Leif skips out of his way, running straight towards the water. He barely avoids Vlad's grasping hands as he dives in.

Sylvia waits beside me, smiling as my gaze connects with hers. "Come on, Mir. We want to play chicken!"

Sighing, I stand from the chair and shed my damp robe. The splashing noises from the pool cease suddenly, leaving a deafening silence in their wake. My eyes slowly drift to the guys and find all of them mid-splash staring in my direction.

I scan across Alex, Marc, and Leif, finally connecting with Vlad's sizzling amber gaze. My cheeks heat with all the attention focused on me and the stupid, tiny swimsuit. Taking a page from Sylvia's book, I run to the water and yell, "Cannonball!"

I surface seconds before Sylvia plunges into the water nearby. Twisting away to avoid the splash, I run straight into Leif. His warm palms grab onto my upper arms as he offers me a wry grin. "You look good in the pool, Mira Love," he states.

A low, rumbling growl sounds behind me. Then, I'm swept into Vlad's arms. His normal ocean and pine scent is covered by the smell of chlorine, but I'm able to recognize his hold.

"Are we playing chicken or what?" He asks.

"I call Marc as my bottom," Sylvia exclaims.

Vlad gently sets me on the edge of the pool. "Do you want to play?"

Grinning, I nod. "We can't let them show us up!"

He releases a rumbling laugh, then helps me to climb onto his shoulders. Vlad easily walks us towards Sylvia and Marc in the six-foot deep section of the pool.

"Yaahhhh," echoes across the backyard before we reach them. Leif comes barreling into view with Alex on his shoulders. The pair easily knocks Sylvia and Marc over.

"Victory," Alex shouts, raising his fists in the air.

The sight of Alex on Leif's shoulders, combined

with Sylvia and Marc's bewildered faces as they splutter in the water, has both Vlad and I doubled over in laughter. And it feels good.

For the first time in a while, all the stress of the curse has faded away. I feel like a normal teenage girl, playing in the pool with her friends.

11

THE REVEAL

Mirabella

Despite the strenuous weeks we've endured recently, I find myself awake in the early morning hours before the sun has crested the horizon. Vlad peppers the silence with steady snores as he sleeps soundly beside me. I attempt to focus on the noise as my gaze traces imaginary patterns on the clean, white ceiling of the room we're sharing, but sleep continues to evade me.

Giving up, I cautiously wriggle from his hold and slip out into the hall with no particular destination in mind. I stop by the bathroom two doors away, then continue down the staircase to the kitchen. My steps falter as a figure standing in the unlit room catches my attention. The light from the moon flashes off a head of blonde hair and I feel my shoulders relax.

I squint slightly before asking, "Alex?"

Although the twins are identical, it's easy to spot their differences. Or at least it usually is. The dim lighting has me less sure of this twin's identity. Until he twirls around and a set of green eyes connect with mine. Alex.

He gives me a probing look, his eyes searching for unknown answers. Shaking his head, he offers a wry grin. "Hey Mira. Can't sleep?"

I wordlessly shake my head and step closer as he lifts a mug from the counter, taking a long sip of the beverage. When I reach the island, he offers the drink to me. "Tea? It's laced with a mild sleeping potion. It will probably help you get some rest."

I hesitate briefly, then accept his offering. "Did Leif brew the potion for you?" I ask, bringing the ceramic surface to my lips for a sip. Sniffing lightly, I smell hints of jasmine and another herb I can't identify. My grandmother would be pleased to know I'm drinking tea, even without her pressuring me. The thought brings a smile to my lips, one that's amplified by the pleasant taste of the liquid as it hits my tongue. It's sweet, but soothing.

"No, I brewed it myself," Alex replies with a shrug.

I work hard to keep the liquid inside my mouth, swallowing it swiftly to avoid spitting it back into the mug or all over Alex. The action was a mistake, however, as the tea travels down the wrong pipe and causes me to choke. I gasp for breath as tea slides down my windpipe.

Alex snags the mug from my hand and places it on the counter, then thwacks his palm against my back. I wave my hand in the air, trying to tell him I'm okay as the last few coughs trickle out of my throat. My eyes are watering by the time I finish coughing enough to inhale deeply.

I suck in air as Alex asks, "Are you okay?"

"Yes," I wheeze out. Clearing my throat a couple times, I take another sip of the tea. This one goes down smoothly and helps ease the ache from violently coughing. "Can you explain how you brewed a potion?" I ask, returning to the issue at hand and hoping to breeze past the whole trying-to-breathe-tea incident.

Alex shrugs. "Yeah, it's a pretty simple one. I can brew it with you sometime, if you're interested."

My brow furrows with confusion. I feel like my brain is short circuiting as I process his words. "You're... you're a witch?" I ask.

He chuckles at my expression and shakes his head. "Yeah. When a witch and a shifter mate it usually results in twins, one of each species. Marc is the shifter, and I'm the witch."

So many things slot into place with his words. Why Alex knew so much about the Curse, the reason behind him accompanying me to my witches exams, his family owning an extensive supernatural archive, even the MMA potion the twins were drinking in Haven. Once I found out that Marc was a shifter, I clumped him and Alex into the same category. I'm only realizing, just now, that I never even asked if my assumptions were correct.

"What?" A distraught voice whispers, echoing across the silent kitchen and interrupting our conversation before I'm able to organize my thoughts into a response.

I twirl around in surprise, my hand flying to grip onto Alex's arm, nails digging in lightly as I seek the owner of the voice. My eyes land on Leif standing at the end of the hall, barely visible in a sliver of moonlight. His face is crestfallen, like we just spoiled Christmas by telling him that that Santa isn't real.

"Leif? Is everything okay?" I ask, wondering why he looks so distraught.

He steps closer, his eyes a million miles away. When he reaches the island, he appears to have buried whatever feeling had upset him, and his face shutters. "My sister was in love with a shifter," he says quietly.

He doesn't meet our eyes, as he settles into a barstool, and I'm unsure whether he plans to say more. I look to Alex, but his expression is equally bewildered. Leif can act strange, but this is extra weird behavior from him.

A pair of muddy brown eyes connect with mine, and I see a flash of pain as he continues. "My father was against the match from the start. He discouraged us from befriending shifters. To him commingling was unconscionable, but my sister didn't, doesn't, share his opinion."

His words pause and I step forward to place a palm lightly against his arm. In comfort, or maybe encouragement. Leif lays a hand over mine, the warmth seeping into my skin as my ears soak up his words.

"My father has always expected us to continue our strong bloodline by marrying legacy witches. He forbid my sister from having a relationship with a shifter because they had no future. Witches and Shifters cannot have children, or if they do, their babies are magical duds. At least according to him."

The ticking of a clock is the only sound audible in the kitchen as his words fade. I suddenly recall Leif's shouted words the day he left Florence after attacking me. As everything slots into place, I feel a bone-deep sadness for Leif and his sister. Their father is a cruel man and a liar. I refuse to believe that the wise Coven Leader, Archibald Golden didn't know the truth about witch and shifter relationships.

Leif interrupts my thoughts as he continues revealing his sister's story riddled by his father's deceit. "Annika... she didn't even care. Unfortunately, that just made our father more aggressive in his mission to sabotage her relationship. He pushed her boyfriend to the brink, ensuring his shifter instincts were constantly triggered at inopportune times. Eventually it became too much. When he finally shifted..." He shrugs, like we all know what happened next and unfortunately, we do.

"He's out there somewhere, as a wolf?" I ask, as a tear leaks out of my eye. Poor Annika. And that poor shifter.

Leif nods as his thumb softly swipes at the moisture on my cheek. My breath catches in my throat at the mournful look on his face. I decide then, at that very moment, to devote my entire life to finding the cure. I have no words that can comfort Leif or his sister after their father's lies and betrayal, but I can find a way to make it right, and I will.

Launching myself at Leif, I wrap my arms tightly around him, squeezing him in the tightest hug that I can. He slowly returns the gesture, gripping me against his torso, between his legs. His hand sweeps down my back in a soothing motion, comforting me as much as I meant to comfort him.

Vlad's sleep-addled voice rumbles through the kitchen. "What's going on? Why the hell are you all awake at three in the morning?"

I jump out of Leif's arms, startled. My cheeks heat like I'm guilty of more than just a hug. My eyes flash to Alex briefly then connect with Vlad's. "None of us could sleep... Since I've been down here though, I've learned two interesting pieces of information we need to share with the others."

I'm thinking of Annika's story and Alex's abilities, but I also haven't discussed my conversation with

Archibald Golden with anyone besides Vlad. Secrets are being unveiled left and right, and I know we need to have a conversation as a group, and soon.

If we're going to work as a team, we all need to possess the same information.

Vlad nods, but remains silent. He aims a glare in Leif's direction as he slings an arm around me, tugging my body against his side.

"Are you guys having a party?" Marc asks, ambling towards the kitchen wearing nothing but a pair of low-slung sweatpants. He yawns loudly, rubbing his eyes with his fists, clearing away sleep.

"Should we just wake up Sylvia?" I ask, glancing around.

Alex's shoulders droop, and he tosses the contents of his mug into the sink. He sighs deeply and states, "Yeah. I'll make some coffee."

12

THE TRYST

Mirabella

Breakfast with the Sieves passes in a blur. I'm barely able to keep my face from falling into my eggs after such a long, sleepless night. The sacrifice was necessary, but the lack of sleep is especially brutal in the early morning hours. The Sieves don't seem to notice their house guests all lack pep and sport under-eye bags as they're too busy regaling us with tales of the twin's past.

Returning to the guest house afterwards, I trudge inside with a nap in mind. Hopefully, I'll be better rested before we eat with the Sieves again. Then I'll be in the right state of mind to snag a few pictures of the twins as kids. For future teasing and blackmail opportunities.

Instead of immediately heading to bed, I detour to

the kitchen. The lack of sleep has transitioned into a pounding headache and I desperately need water and ibuprofen. I open a few cupboards before finding the glasses, then turn to the sink and fill my cup with tap water. After a couple sips, my brain seems a little less angry. Turning to the pantry, I search the lower shelves, then perch on my tiptoes as I hunt for miracle-cure medicine.

"Little Mir."

The words are whispered directly behind my left ear. Surprise causes me to lose my balance and I almost tip face forward into shelves laden with snacks. Vlad's quick reflexes catch me. His arms wrap around my waist, tugging my back against his front, and saving me from a snack catastrophe.

He tucks his nose into the crook of my neck, inhaling deeply. I expect him to release me, but he peppers my neck with soft, light kisses, instead. I sigh and lean into him further, only to have a rock-hard erection press against my spine.

"I have a surprise for you," Vlad whispers between kisses.

I chuckle, then murmur back, "If I can feel it, is it still a surprise?"

"What?" Vlad asks. He stops his kisses and gently pushes against my shoulder to twirl me around. Our eyes connect and I notice the confusion in his amber gaze almost immediately.

My cheeks heat as I realize he was not attempting to dirty talk me.

He processes my words seconds later and releases a deep, belly laugh. His gaze turns heated, and he rakes a quick glance down my body. Leaning closer he whispers, "That wasn't exactly the surprise I had in mind, but it can be, if you want."

Giggling to cover my extreme mortification, I playfully push against his shoulder. "Tell me the real surprise first. Maybe that can come later."

A smirk graces his plump lips, and he tangles a hand in my hair. His face tips forward and he places a light kiss against my mouth. Angling my head to kiss across my jaw, he ends his trail underneath my ear.

I tug against his hold seeking an actual kiss, instead of his soft teasing ones. Vlad receives the unspoken message and hovers above my mouth for a brief pause. Then, our lips collide in a searing kiss. His tongue lashes against mine as he claims my mouth.

Vlad uses every tool at his disposal to completely devour me. I lose myself to the drugging sensation, leaning into him completely. It ends too quickly, and I release an embarrassing whimper as he pulls away.

"There can be more of that later," he whispers, releasing my hair and intertwining our fingers instead. "I want to take you to your surprise, but first we need to grab a few things."

. . .

THE FIRST PART of Vlad's surprise is a red convertible, the second part is a long, mysterious drive in the vehicle. "Will you tell me where we're going now?" I ask for the seventeenth time, as the wind whips through my air.

Vlad chuckles, reaching across the console to squeeze my palm. "Do you hate surprises, Little Mir?" He asks. His rumbling voice, combined with the mystery of what is coming, causes my stomach to do backflips.

I briefly shake my head in response, even though I'd rather be the one surprising, then the one being surprised. Instead of pestering Vlad, again, and receiving a lack of answers, again, I focus out the space where the window normally sits and watch the scenery blur by.

Vlad effortlessly winds the vehicle down a twisty road leading towards the water. The houses become more elaborate and spaced further apart, indicating we've entered a wealthy neighborhood.

The style of the homes reminds me of Florence in a way, and a pang of homesickness strikes me suddenly. Inhaling a deep breath, I force myself to bury the feeling before it leads me in a downward spiral of depression.

We drive past the last house, onto a peninsula reaching out into the ocean like an extended hand. The road transitions from paved to gravel. Vlad reduces his speed to avoid spraying us with the small pebbles through the open windows and top, which gives me extra time to check out the views.

The land is peppered with trees, providing shadow over the road. The sturdy oaks are set far enough apart that the water is visible half a mile or so past the road on either side.

Vlad pulls up to a modest, pale-blue home, rolling to a stop and shutting off the ignition.

"Where are we?" I whisper, twisting my head to absorb the scenery and peaceful silence.

There hasn't been another house in miles. The only noises are the lap of the water against the shore and the peaceful chirping of birds.

My gaze finally connects with Vlad's and he smirks in response. He exits the car and rounds the front without uttering a word. When he reaches my door, he opens it and offers me his hand. I grab onto his palm as curiosity eats me alive. I want, no need, to know why Vlad brought me here and is acting so mysterious.

He pauses near a clean, white door, and fiddles with a lockbox attached to the handle until it opens and reveals a key. Inserting it into the lock, he squeezes my hand gently, then pushes the door inwards to reveal a simple and homey interior.

Ashy wooden floors spread throughout the house, complemented by pale gray walls. Simple, comfortable looking furniture is scattered throughout the home. It's the epitome of a beach cottage and I love it.

Tugging against Vlad's hand, I attempt to drag him

through the living room to check out the bedroom, but he remains rooted in place. I shoot him an irritated glance, and he chuckles in response.

"Patience, Little Mir. We can check out the rest of the house soon. I have something I want to show you first."

He swiftly yanks on my hand, catching me off guard and sending me tumbling into his chest. Vlad wraps an arm around my waist as I regain my footing. He uses the connection to steer me straight down the hallway and through a simple wooden door with paned glass at the rear of the house.

The moment we step outside, I'm speechless.

A concrete patio expands a couple dozen feet off the back of the house, dropping off when it reaches sand littered with small pebbles. Beyond that, water laps against the shore, creating a peaceful, steady cadence. I turn my head to look at Vlad, wanting to express how wonderful the house is, when a flash of red catches my attention.

Directly to Vlad's right, red rose petals are scattered across the ground in a line, leading to a set of patio chairs. Across from the chairs sits an easel, already holding a blank canvas, accompanied by a small table covered in containers of paints and miscellaneous brushes. Past the cozy painting nook sits a set of open French doors leading back to the house. The ground there is littered with more petals, spreading inside, out of my line of sight.

Twisting in Vlad's grip, I meet his amber gaze and softly ask, "Did you do all this for me?"

Vlad smirks as he replies, "Of course. Would you like to see where the rest of the flowers lead, Little Mir?"

Wordlessly, I nod my head while still gazing into his eyes. Vlad has a hard-outer shell, but the more time I spend with him, the more I find he has a truly kind heart hidden underneath. A heart that I find myself falling for more deeply with each passing day.

With our eyes locked, I lift onto my toes, attempting to bring my face closer to his, but I fall short by a few inches. Releasing a chuckle, he tilts forward, meeting me halfway. Our lips collide in a passionate exchange of unspoken feelings.

While his lips, teeth, and tongue claim me, searing heat down to my very core, my mouth brands his soul with my name. The exchange stops time, and everything in the background fades away as Vlad becomes the sole center of my existence.

Vlad eventually ends the kiss, groaning while he tears his lips from mine, as if the experience physically pains him. His eyes search mine as he returns to stand to his full height, towering above me.

Wrapping his arm around my waist once more, he tucks me into his side and mutters, "We will continue that soon, but I want you to see the rest, first."

Giggling at his reluctant tone, I allow him to lead me towards the French doors and into a modest bedroom dominated by a king-sized bed. It appears as if a bouquet of red roses exploded within the room, coating the white bedspread and floor in fragrant petals.

Sitting amidst the remnants of colorful blooms, in the center of the bed, is a tray holding an ice bucket. It's cooling a bottle, with a glass resting on either side. Stepping forward, away from Vlad, I snag the bottled beverage to read the label.

My eyebrows raise in surprise and I ask, "You bought champagne?"

"There's no pressure or expectations about tonight, but I thought we deserved some time away from the group. To be alone."

I stifle the laugh attempting to bubble up as I think about the group of cockblocks we've left behind at the Sieves.

Vlad continues unaware of my thoughts. "I want to spend time with you. In bed, or in the kitchen, or on the patio, watching you paint. I know how much you love your art and I feel you've been forced to abandon it while we've searched for a cure. Tonight is a night for us to be ourselves, Little Mir."

My heart swells with each word he utters. This sweet, caring, thoughtful man has created the perfect escape from the chaos surrounding us lately. I'm unable to form a response, despite, or maybe because of, the massive amount of gratitude flooding through my veins.

After a lengthy pause, Vlad sounds less sure of himself as he asks, "Is this too much? Do you not like it?"

I decline with a shake of my head and launch myself at him, clinging onto his body with my arms and legs like a spider monkey. Vlad releases a surprised chuckle, but captures me in his hold. His palms grip onto my bottom as he hoists me upwards, allowing me to wrap my arms around his neck.

"I absolutely love it," I whisper.

Vlad seals his lips to mine with his next breath, walking us to the bed a couple feet away. He bends over, maintaining his hold and our kiss as my back hits the mattress covered in petals. He breaks our kiss and I whimper as his warm body leaves mine.

"Patience, Little Mir," he teases.

I grunt in frustration, moving to rest against my elbows on the mattress, enabling a better view of him. My eyes trace his movements as he removes the tray with champagne, then yanks his shirt over his head in one smooth motion. I drink in Vlad's broad pecs and defined abs, my gaze flitting down to his narrow waist, and landing on his jeans.

He wordlessly rejoins me on the bed. Seeking permission in my eyes, he slides his fingers under the hem of my shirt and gently tugs it over my head. Once the clothing is removed, our mouths connect again in a fiery kiss. The motion of his lips is drugging and I barely register his movements as he removes his jeans, then helps me to shimmy out of the rest of my clothing.

Panting for breath, we separate. Vlad's hands drift down my naked body as he explores my skin. He starts by rubbing them over my shoulders, then down my arms, returning to cup my breasts. With one hand he tweaks and rubs my right nipple, while his mouth descends on my left. Sensations immediately bombard me and I arch into the contact, as I lose myself in the pleasure.

Vlad's hand continues to roam, sliding down my belly until they reach the apex of my thighs. His mouth changes from my left nipple to my right as Vlad slips a single finger inside my pussy.

I moan at the contact, and he uses my liquid heat to lube his finger before adding another. My next moan is a combination of pleasure and pain as he stretches me out slightly.

Hearing my distress, his fingers leave to find the sensitive bundle of nerves at my core. He slides his fingers slick with my desire over my nub, ramping up the sensations until my muscles seize. Vlad lifts his head, his amber eyes connecting with mine and in seconds, I fall over the edge as my orgasm rips through me.

Vlad drags me slightly further up the bed before settling between my legs. His eyes connect with mine in question. I nod, and he slowly slides in. His enormous erection stretches me until I feel like I'm going to break.

My body tenses slightly and Vlad pauses. His mouth returns to my breasts, reigniting my pleasure. My core floods with heat and I arch up into him. Vlad withdraws to the tip of his cock, sliding it back in inch by inch.

The sting fades by the time he's fully sheathed and I find myself encouraging him to speed up with my ankles pushing against his back. Vlad quickly slides out and slams back in, while I rise to meet him for each thrust. He places his hand underneath my bottom, changing the angle and the new spot he hits brings my pleasure to a whole new level.

He continues to thrust inside me as my pussy tightens around him, each thrust driving me higher and higher until another orgasm tears through me. Vlad groans as the aftershocks of pleasure extend while he continues to thrust inside me, then he stills with a deep grunt.

His eyes lock with mine and he leans down, sealing his lips to mine in a searing, claiming kiss that conveys his feelings.

"You're perfect, Little Mir."

AFTER CUDDLING TOGETHER on the bed, and dozing on and off for some time, I wriggle in Vlad's grasp. He squeezes me briefly before reluctantly relinquishing his hold. As I sit upright, I notice an open door across from the bed revealing a closet with two robes hanging inside.

Padding over with bare feet, I take the significantly smaller one, clearly meant for me. Once it's tied around my body, I glance at Vlad. His amber gaze connects with mine and he winks, but makes no move to leave the bed.

"Is it okay if I paint?" I ask, not wanting to abandon him, but my fingers itching to fill the bare canvas waiting outside, all the same.

"Go ahead, I'll join you in a few," he replies.

Nodding, I leave the bedroom, stepping through the open doors into the cool ocean air. The sun has just begun to set, bathing everything in sight with a pinky orange hue. Inhaling a deep breath of the clean air, I stare at the beautiful surroundings for a few minutes, then get to work.

My hands work swiftly, pouring colors and selecting brushes, dipping one into the paint before I've had a single, conscious thought about how I want to cover the canvas. The brush flies across the empty expanse of space, creating outlines in a soft, black paint, then shading in the shadows. I'm interrupted briefly when a champagne flute appears at the edge of my line of sight.

Glancing up, I find Vlad offering the glass with a slight smile. I accept it, pausing to sip champagne for the first time. The bubbly liquid fizzles and pops as it coats my tongue, leaving a light, but sweet flavor in its wake.

"This is really good," I say softly, my eyes tracking Vlad's movements as he settles into one of the chairs behind my easel, his body clad in the other robe.

"I'm glad you like it," he replies. "Keep painting, I want to watch you create."

Nodding, I take another sip, then set the glass on my paint table. My eyes return to the canvas and I see a bunch of black slashes, no clear images formed yet.

Inhaling deeply, I pick up another brush. I sling paint across the canvas until every inch of previously blank space is splashed with color. Then, I set my brush in a cup of now murky water and snag my champagne glass.

As I step back, I hear rustling, indicating Vlad is leaving his chair to join me. I'm too distracted by my painting to acknowledge him. At first, my brows furrow in confusion at the image until suddenly it clicks. Vlad and I turn to face each other in sync.

"We need to get back to the others," I whisper.

13

THE PREMONITION

Mirabella

Vlad flies down the road at a rapid pace, the red convertible taking corners like a NASCAR vehicle. With his lead foot and sharp turns, we're able to make it back to the Sieves in half the time it took to reach the beach cottage.

The sun has fully set, and the house is dark besides a few lights peppering the driveway and porch. Vlad silently shuts off the car and I hear my heartbeat pounding in my ears.

We exchange a glance fraught with more meaning than any we've shared previously. I read regret, adoration, and determination in his gaze. My eyes multiply the emotions and reciprocate them. Conveying my feelings over our night ending too soon, dedication to our friends, and the cure that feels closer to our grasp than ever before.

With a slow nod, I yank open the door and rush into the guest house. Not wanting to waste my time running around and gathering my friends, I stop in the center of the living room and screech, "Everyone downstairs, now!"

A stampede of feet responds and within seconds, the group filters into the room from various directions, slowly forming a semi-circle around me. Alex is the last to arrive. He has a manic energy wafting off him and appears to still be wearing the clothes from brunch. It doesn't look like he's slept at all. Or at least if he has, he hasn't changed.

The second he joins the group, his gaze snaps to Leif, and he asks, "Did you already tell them?"

"No, we were waiting for everyone to arrive," He replies dryly. I drag my attention away from Alex to watch as Leif rises from an armchair to lean against the wall, closer to the rest of us. "Now that you're here, we can start."

Before Alex can respond, Marc steps in, "Mira, Vlad, it's good you came back early. We started searching for answers after you left, not wanting to waste any of the time we have here. As you know, our parents have been archiving since before our birth. Their parents archived before them and so on. It's part of our family's legacy. Anyway, there's something we want to show you in the library. We think that it's important."

Vlad and I exchange a glance, and I nod. If they found something significant, we need to check it out. We can't continue with only half the group having information, and the other half being in the dark. For this to work, we need to collectively work together as a group to break the curse.

My announcement can wait. I hope.

Marc leads us to the main home, through the French doors facing the guest house. As a group, we trail behind him, veering left down a long hallway. I catch glimpses of impressive rooms filled with antique furniture, but Marc's pace doesn't leave time to examine anything too closely.

If we weren't in a race against time, and possibly covens of evil witches, I would beg for the opportunity to wander through each room at my leisure. Considering our current situation, I settle myself with the brief snapshots. I also hold onto the hope that after this is all over, if it ever is, I'll be able to return to Connecticut and experience the Sieves house for real.

I'm so lost in thought, I slam into Marc as he stops. Bouncing off his back, I'm captured by a pair of familiar muscular arms. Instead of releasing me, Vlad carries me like a rag doll the rest of the way to our destination.

When Marc pushes a pair of dark oak doors open at the end of the hall, I'm instantly grateful I'm not on my own two feet. If I were, I probably would've fallen over in awe. My jaw drops as my head swivels left and right to examine the room.

Rows of navy colored bookshelves are arranged across the floor in straight lines. Each shelf contains books upon books, spanning as far as my eye can see. Golden lamps create a soft glow in the expansive space, giving the room a peaceful, and slightly forbidden ambience.

Vlad slowly slides my body down his, gently releasing me as my feet tap against the floor. My body urges me to gasp, but I swallow the sound, not wanting to disturb the silence coating the room.

I turn to my right and find Marc and Alex both watching me. They look even more alike than usual, wearing identical, soft smiles. Past the twins sits a table covered in books with several plush arm chairs circled around it.

"Is this the archives?" I whisper, spinning around, attempting to see everything, all at once.

"Well, this is our collection of books," Alex answers. He grasps onto my elbow and steers me to the far corner of the room. Situated on a small desk is a sleek looking computer set-up. "This is the archives."

I glance at the computer, eyes widening further in shock. This is like the world-wide witching web all over again. I guess witches have really embraced the twenty-first century.

"May I?" I ask, gesturing to the chair.

"Of course," Alex replies with a smile. "I think you'll find the database is similar to ones we use at work..."

"We've identified all the legacies," Sylvia shouts, cutting off the rest of Alex's sentence.

I pause, with my legs bent and my bottom halfway to the seat cushion. "What? Why didn't you lead with that? I don't even need the archives now. Why are we even in here?" I ask, glancing around again.

Alex shrugs, appearing sheepish. "Sorry, you were so entranced, I got caught up in the moment and... forgot I guess."

Sylvia shoves him out of the way. He glares at her, but I can see a bit of sibling-like affection, making it more for show than anything else. Sylvia grabs my hand and drags me to the table surrounded by chairs.

Sitting amidst stacks of haphazard books appears to be two lineage trees jotted down on pieces of thick parchment paper. The first is labeled with a large "S" and the second with a large "W"

"We labeled them, but didn't want to put too much information... in case they get into the wrong hands," Sylvia explains, answering my unasked question.

I nod, leaning forward to look at the charts. My eyes skim down each column on the "W" page. The first ends in my name, which we all already knew. The second shows Leif, but the third and fourth have my eyebrows raising into my hairline.

Turning my head, I catch Sylvia's gaze and she

nods once. Next, I look at Alex and he shrugs. "Did either of you know?" I ask.

Sylvia shakes her head, but also replies, "My parents mentioned something one time about 'our legacy' but I didn't realize they meant 'We are legacies'. I thought it was more of an expression. You know how my parents are though... they're more free-spirited than anything else and they probably couldn't care less if their kids were legacies or if we were magical duds."

I nod in acceptance of her answer, then turn to Alex.

"Our parents shunned a lot of the witching traditions after they mated. My mom taught me magic, but she rarely talks about the past or her family."

"It's all a little strange," I murmur. While storing the word 'mated' in the back of my mind for a future conversation with Vlad.

My eyes return to the page as my thoughts run wild. I barely register the letters passing by as I skim the last column to read the name of the fifth and final witch legacy. My brow furrows as I try to think of anyone I know named Gregory.

For some reason, the last name on the page sounds more familiar than the first. The name Gregory doesn't immediately ring a bell and once it does, it's perhaps the most perplexing. "Gregory Fink... as in Kaylee's Greg?" I finally ask.

"The one and hopefully only," Sylvia replies.

My eyes skim the parchment again, but nothing has changed. "Do you think it's a little odd?"

"The list of legacies?" Sylvia asks.

"No, that we all seem to have been drawn together... as if by magic."

"Except Gregory, err Greg," she replies pointing to the parchment.

"Well, actually that's not exactly true. The day I was summoned to the Coven building and warned against talking about the Shifters, Greg approached me in the parking lot before heading into the building. He asked me if we could meet up to discuss..." I reply, only to be interrupted by a growl randomly ripping out of Vlad's throat.

I look at him in question, wondering if he's upset over Greg, only to find his gaze is fixated on the table. Curious about what set him off, I follow his line of sight to look at the "S" parchment. Skimming down the column I find the first name and find Marc, which I guess isn't too surprising.

My eyebrow raises at the next name, Tony Martinez. But it's the last name that Vlad is clearly reacting to.

It's his.

Vlad straightens his spine and wordlessly walks towards the door. His movements are stiff and disjointed, like he can barely control his body.

Concern floods my veins and I move to follow, but Marc waves me off with a gentle smile. He exits the room and breaks into a light jog, catching up with Vlad before he rounds the corner and disappears from view.

I drag my eyes away from the empty hallway to meet Sylvia's sympathetic gaze. She steps forward and wraps her arm around my shoulders. "He'll be okay, Mir."

"Yeah," I agree lightly.

Honestly, I'm not sure if Vlad will be able to fully process the reveal of his parent's names and his legacy status anytime soon. These past few months have been hard on all of us. But Vlad is not doing well with learning more about his birth parents on top of everything else. At least, not if storming out of the room in a fit of unadulterated rage is any indication of his feelings.

Instead of dwelling on things I can't change, I wrap an arm around Sylvia, then pivot us to face Alex and Leif. "What should we do while we wait?"

"There are a few board games in here. Is anyone down for a game of Monopoly?" Alex suggests.

"I am the queen of Monopoly. You are going down," Sylvia crows. She releases my shoulders and moves towards the table.

Together, she and Leif stack the legacy lists to the side while Alex wanders off to grab the board game. I watch my friends in pensive silence, my thoughts drifting back to the list of legacies.

My friends found the information hours prior and

have had time to process it. Versus I have had mere minutes to think about the names.

"C'mon Mir," Sylvia shouts, startling me out of my thoughts.

Glancing up, I see Alex, Leif and Sylvia have already settled around the table. Leif has acquired a small, white visor and is setting money into four separate stacks.

Relaxing my tense shoulders, I pull out a chair and ask, "What's with the hat?"

Leif glares at me briefly before returning his attention to the money to continue counting. "Why has everyone asked that? It's the banker visor, the banker always wears it."

"Okay, now ask where it came from," Sylvia mock-whispers from my left.

Grinning, I ask, "Where did the visor come from?"

Leif releases a bone-weary sigh. "I always carry around a small assortment of potions. You already know that, Mira."

"You carry around a potion for a banker visor?" I barely maintain a straight face while asking the question. Sylvia completely loses it, releasing a cackle as Leif's cheeks tinge with pink.

Instead of answering, Leif shoves a stack of colorful paper money in my direction. "Let's roll to see who's first."

. . .

While we wait for the two shifters to return from their run, and play a very competitive game of Monopoly, I waffle about whether to reveal my news now or once we're all back together.

We just had a heart to heart the other day where we adamantly agreed on no more secrets, but the only person who would temporarily be out of the loop is Marc.

Inhaling deeply, I release my breath slowly until each ounce of air has left my lungs. I'm hoping my friends don't think I'm crazy after I say what I need to. My brain tries to think of stall tactics, wanting to delay this statement, but I force my lips to blurt, "I think I'm painting the future."

Sylvia gasps, and the boys simply stare. Leif finally gestures, waving a hand and the air and says, "Go on."

"Okay, so it all started with paintings of wolves, primarily Vlad's wolf before I knew anything about magic or shifters…"

Sylvia gasps again, then murmurs, "Your painting of Candy Land. It wasn't Candy Land… It was Haven!"

I nod slowly. I'm grateful that Sylvia's belief in me is full and immediate. I don't know why I doubted this group of people, who have supported me from the beginning. I assumed they would question something seemingly impossible, but that isn't really their style. After all, we've been facing the seemingly impossible together all summer.

"There may have been others, ones that I didn't even realize. I know you can't remember your time in Haven, but when I was in the archives, I drew an image of the bookcases falling like dominos. It was maybe a mere hour later when Alex and Marc made the image come to life. Then there's also this."

I pull my phone from my pocket and open the images app to the most recent picture taken. One of my canvases from the beach cottage. Flipping my phone around, I show the photo to my three friends seated nearby. "I painted this a few hours ago…" I allow them a few minutes to look at the painting and come to their own conclusions before I continue.

Leif is the first to respond, "You know what we need to do?"

Nodding, I reply, "We need to wait for Marc and Vlad to get back. Then, we need a plan to collect the rest of the legacies."

Sylvia nods firmly, then she states, "Whatever it is, you know I'm in." Then she turns her attention to Leif. "Also, that's my property and you owe me $100.00 for landing there."

Leif groans, counting out a paper stack of money and placing it in Sylvia's outstretched palm. During their transaction, Alex scoots his chair closer to mine and snags my hand off the table. "We're going to figure this out, Mira. For my brother and Vlad, plus all the other shifters out there. We can do it."

I meet his steady emerald gaze and allow his confidence to infuse me. I nod in response and squeeze his palm. "I hope you're right," I whisper.

14

THE PLAN

Mirabella

The second Marc and Vlad return from their run, the guest house becomes a flurry of activity. The shifters run upstairs to freshen up, while Alex scurries away to grab some pens and pads of paper. Sylvia is scrolling social media and shouting things at innocent people posting about their lives, which seems to be her method of stress relief. I stand near the kitchen watching as Leif methodically pops six bags of popcorn, for no apparent reason.

Eventually the chaos mellows out. We all settle around the coffee table in the living room, holding our own personal bags of popcorn, courtesy of Leif. In the center of the table sits the two parchments, and an assortment of notebooks and pens.

After we fill in Marc, the only sound in the room is

the crunch of popcorn. Every eye in the room is fixated on the coffee table, like the parchment paper will suddenly grow a mouth and spew wisdom on what we should do next.

Unfortunately, after a solid half hour and six bags of popcorn later, the documents from the coffee table still haven't spoken.

"Okay—"

"What if—"

"We should—"

The previously silent room suddenly fills with clashing voices as Leif, Alex, and I blurt out ideas simultaneously.

"You can start Mira Love," Leif states.

Smiling lightly, I begin. "Okay, so we know we need the other two legacies. The easiest course of action would be to simply go to Florence and collect them."

"Either by coercion or willing cooperation," Vlad rumbles out.

My eyes soak in his grim expression as I meet his amber gaze. Turbulent emotions are apparent in his eyes, likely lingering from the revelations of earlier this evening. Despite his feelings about the matter, he's clearly tabled the issue for now, so I force myself to do the same until there's time to talk in private.

"What about Mir?" Sylvia asks, directing the question at the entire group. "She can't go back after what happened last time. Honestly, I'm not sure that any of us will be safe if we return. What if they have some witchy task force out looking for us?"

"Even if we were safe to return, what do we do after we gather the other legacies?" Alex asks.

A thread of thought nags at my consciousness, teasing me with its elusiveness. I miss part of the conversation as I attempt to search the deepest caverns of my mind, knowing I have the answer to this question.

Suddenly, I recall the painting in Hope. As grim as it was, I think it holds the answer to the future. "We need to go back to the Spring. Together, with all the legacies," I whisper.

My words halt the conversation continuing around me. Alex is the first to respond, "The Spring? That was a dead end."

I shake my head forcefully to decline. "I painted it. I think it's the next step, after we're all together. Once we're there, maybe more answers will come to us."

A wave of nods slowly drifts across the circle as each of my friends consider my response and accept it.

"I don't think we should split up, but Sylvia is right. I think I'm on the Coven's most wanted list, if that exists. The rest of you could probably fly under the radar long enough to grab the legacies, but I definitely don't think I can," I state.

"You can't go somewhere by yourself, that isn't safe," Alex replies.

"What if we all went to Florence, but you just laid

low somewhere? That way if anything goes wrong, we're not spread out all over the place. We'll be in one concentrated area. We'll be able to react to any problems quicker that way, also," Marc suggests.

I open my mouth to reply, but I'm interrupted by Leif. "I know a potion that can help. Can you gather some brewing supplies? I have a list of ingredients..."

We stand in the Sieves portal room the next afternoon. Each of us holding a vial of potion meant to disguise our appearance.

If the situation wasn't so perilous, I would be freaking out with Sylvia about how cool this whole magic thing is. Because the skilled potions are So. Fricken. Cool. Instead of verbalizing my excitement, I internalize a few fan-girl type screams. I throw in some jazz hands, hoping there will be a better situation to celebrate with my bestie in the near future.

"Where should we have the portal drop us?" Leif asks as we stare at the empty doorframe.

"I think we should have it drop us at my grandma's house," I reply immediately. "Vlad and I can wait there for the rest of you and there's a portal in case we need to leave in a hurry."

"Are your cars still there? Or were they returned to your houses?" Sylvia asks in response.

Crap. I didn't even think of that.

"I haven't talked to anyone. Should I text my grandma?" I ask.

"I don't know if we want communication out there that we're coming," Alex chimes in. "I would hate to think the conspiracy goes far enough that our phone records are being tracked or bugged, but if they are…"

"Why don't we go to my house? Or the woods behind my house," Vlad suggests, cutting Alex off. "We can check and make sure no one is watching from the tree line prior to heading inside. If our cars haven't been returned, we can take my parent's car to Mira's grandma's house. Mira and I will wait there, while the rest of you search. If the cars have been returned, you four can borrow my car and stop on the way to grab someone else's. You'll probably need two vehicles to collect the remaining legacies."

A brief pause follows as we consider his words. "My grandma's house is in the middle of nowhere… it would take way more time to get into town on foot from her place if our cars have been moved," I concede.

No one jumps in to disagree. I see a few shrugs and a few nods, which is good enough. If we can't risk communicating with anyone in Florence, Vlad's plan is the most likely to be successful.

"We all know the plan then?" Leif asks after his eyes flit around the room, stopping to land on mine.

"Step one: drink these vials, yell hocus pocus and

jump in the portal. Step two: separate. Marc and I find Tony, while Leif and Alex find Greg. Vlad and Mira wait at Vlad's parent's house. Step three: once the legacies are acquired, we reconvene at Vlad's. Step four: portal out of Mira's grandma's tree," Sylvia states. Then she turns and salutes Leif like he's a militia leader.

"Err, yes," Leif responds, a look of slight confusion apparent on his face.

Sylvia doubles over laughing at his expression. The infectious sound causes me to laugh with her and the mood in the room lightens slightly. Sylvia hiccups a few times before containing her laughter and standing upright. "Sorry, it was just so serious in here. I couldn't help myself."

Shaking my head, I release one last giggle over Sylvia and Leif. Then I uncork my vial. "To the legacies!"

Placing my potion in the middle of our circle, I wait for everyone to clank theirs against mine in a mock cheers. Then I guzzle the liquid down. Once it's emptied, I tuck the vial into my backpack, ready to portal back home.

Leif's gaze scans the room, confirming potions have been consumed. He turns towards the portal and removes another vial from his pocket. Leif dumps the contents on the ground, just inside the empty doorframe, and murmurs something under his breath.

The frame fills with the familiar shimmery screen,

but I don't focus on the progress. Instead, my gaze sweeps across my friends gathered close by, examining their bodies as they transform into their new, temporary appearances.

As part of the brewing process, we had to write a list of our new, desired features and throw it into the bubbling cauldron. My mystified eyes watch as Vlad shrinks, and Sylvia shoots up four inches. Her violet hair transitions to a deep brown, as Alex's nose elongates and forms in a slightly left-leaning hook. Leif's hair transitions into a deep onyx, so dark it refracts the light emanating from the portal. Marc is almost unrecognizable by the time my eyes land on him. He has a thinner build with vibrant blue eyes and soft brown hair, similar to his father's.

I look down at my own body expecting flowing red locks and longer legs, but nothing appears to have changed. "Did mine not work?" I ask, perplexed after seeing the transition of my friends.

Leif chuckles, "Yours definitely worked, Mira Love. You just won't be able to see the changes to yourself. It's part of the potion. The spell distorts you to the viewer's eye, but not to yourself."

His response has me feeling slightly crestfallen. Watching the others ramped up my excitement to see myself as a tall, curvy redhead. Instead of lamenting the unchangeable, I offer a brief nod, then move on. "Is everyone ready?"

"Ready."

"Yep."

"Let's do this."

"Everybody was kung-fu fighting…"

"…Fast as lightening…"

Rolling my eyes, I ignore the twins and snag Vlad's hand. Despite his smaller appearance, his warm palm feels the same as it did prior to drinking the potion. I pull him with me towards the portal. We cross through the thick air simultaneously, rapidly falling towards the hard earth.

This time when we land, we create three separate piles a couple dozen of feet apart, with Leif standing off to the side. As I rise to my feet, brushing off dirt and other miscellaneous forest debris, I ask in a loud-whisper, "Will you please, please, teach us how to do that?"

Leif just smirks and places a finger against his lips in a shushing motion. Vlad rises slowly behind me, gathering my body against his. He places his nose into the crook of my neck and inhales deeply while squeezing me tightly. In my ear he whispers, "It's weird to see you like this, but at least you still smell like you, Little Mir."

The words are lusty and sound like a compliment. White-hot heat streaks through my belly, but I do my best to tamp it down, fighting the urge to trail my hands over his body.

"You smell the same too," I say, instead. And it's true. Despite appearing half a foot shorter, blond, and significantly less toned, Vlad's ocean-pine scent remains reassuringly the same.

"If you two are done smelling each other over there, the coast is clear," Leif calls out. His slightly accented tone making his sarcasm as cutting as the edge of a dagger.

Embarrassment heats my cheeks as Vlad captures my hand and tugs me along with him. He rushes through the empty expanse of grass towards the house. By the time we reach the back door, I'm feeling more optimistic about our plan. At least I'll have the opportunity to spend more time alone with Vlad. The few hours we had at the beach cottage passed too quickly.

Vlad surpasses the rest of the group waiting by the door, dragging me with him by our interconnected palms. He fumbles around the top of the door frame for a few seconds, then places a key into the lock.

Our group swiftly shuffles into the house and out of sight of any nosy neighbors. Alex enters last, slamming the door shut as the rest of us file into the living room. Vlad releases my hand to stride towards the blinds, separating two to peek between them.

"My car is out front. You can use it as one of your vehicles." He removes the keys from a hook near the door and tosses them to Marc.

Marc catches them one handed and nods. "Thanks,

we'll grab mine on the way. Hopefully, we'll find them easily, and one of us will come back to pick you up."

"Should we have brewed some type of potion for you to find them easier?" I ask, thinking of the idea belatedly.

Leif shakes his head. "There is a tracking potion, but it's not very accurate. It can lead you to anywhere a person has been recently, not just where they are currently. Tracking is more closely tied to other types of magic than potions, therefore less effective when used by potions witches."

The ability to track our targets would be convenient today, but as I contemplate Leif's answer, I find that I'm relieved. If tracking potions were simple to use, the Coven would have already tracked us down. If anything, the volatile nature of tracking has probably contributed to our current freedom.

"Okay," I finally whisper. There's no reason to keep quiet, but the stealth required for our situation has me keeping my voice low, regardless. "You know what you need to do. Fly under the radar, find your marks, and complete your mission."

"You make this sound like a spy movie," Alex chuckles.

I shrug, grinning. "Well, it kind of is."

Leif interjects, more somber than the rest of us. "We need to get going. Every minute we're here is another opportunity for someone to catch us, or more specifically Mira Love."

His words immediately sober the group, causing their smiles to drop off. Before my eyes, spines straighten and the air transitions to that of a funeral.

My friends march to the door and as they file out, I whisper, "Good luck, we'll see you soon."

Hopefully.

15

THE RETURN

Mirabella

Vlad and I wait in his room. I pace the floor back and forth until I wear out some of my anxious energy and perch on his bed. The second my butt touches the mattress, I'm hit with the sudden urge to sketch.

Glancing around, I spot a notebook with lined paper on the desk. Pointing to it, I ask, "May I?"

Vlad follows the direction of my finger and smirks. "I'll do you one better." He rises to his feet and opens the top drawer of his desk. He snags a sketchpad and a charcoal pencil, offering me both before he settles into the spot next to me.

I flip the front cover, intent on finding a blank page, only to realize the book is brand new. I sneak a glance at Vlad under my lashes, and find his gaze watching my hands intently, waiting for me to fill the page with an image. It dawns on me that Vlad purchased this book so I would have something to draw in when I come over.

Leaning towards him, I place a chaste kiss against his lips. "Thank you."

Vlad shrugs, seeming embarrassed, so I return my attention to the paper. I allow my mind to wander as the pencil flies across the page. A myriad of gray lines and dark shading begin to appear, as the charcoal tip crosses the paper, slowly turning into shapes before my eyes. I continue to draw until the image feels complete.

Once I fill the first page, I flip to the next and start the process all over again. I draw a series of images until the urge to sketch has relinquished its hold on my fingers. With a relieved sigh, I remove the pencil from the paper to take it all in, flipping back to the beginning. My eyes scan the paper and the feeling of relief evaporates almost immediately.

"Vlad," I say, fear apparent in my words.

He leans forward, his chest resting against my shoulder as he looks at the sketchpad. On the paper is an image of a wolf and a human. They're surrounded and soon to be overwhelmed. On every side stands a cloaked form.

Although the image doesn't say the word danger, the message is clear.

The ominous feeling reminds me of another recent

image. One that I've been shoving deep down into the inaccessible caverns of my brain. The one I drew in Hope. The one that portrayed me dying.

Shaking my head to clear the memory away, I realize Vlad has left the bed. He's pulling aside one small portion of his curtain to look out onto his front lawn, when my eyes touch on his back.

"Fuck," he swears softly, the word barely rumbling across the room to reach my ears.

I scramble off the bed, diving underneath his arm to catch a brief glimpse before the fabric falls back into place. A gasp struggles to break free from my throat, but I quickly stifle it with my hand, worried the noise will give us away.

Vlad seals the curtain to the wall, banishing the lawn from view, but it doesn't matter. I'm replaying the mental image of a swarm of coven witches dressed in black robes storming down the street, a clear mission in mind.

"What do we do?" I ask. I'm attempting to hold back my panic long enough to create a plan.

"Come with me," he replies softly.

Linking our hands, he tugs me down the hall and I stumble over my feet, attempting to take long enough strides to keep up. We reach the kitchen and he releases my palm, moving his hands to my shoulders. He uses the grip to twirl me around.

Face to face, I stare into panicked amber orbs briefly before I realize he's speaking, "... Text the group immediately. Once I'm done shifting, I need you to unlock the door handle and crack the door. Then, I need you to hop on my back. Get as close to my body as possible and hold on tight. Don't look up or let go for any reason, okay?"

Vlad shakes my shoulders when I don't respond immediately. I give a brief nod, even though I'm still processing his rushed instructions, my mind scrambling to understand his words as panic grips me in its claws.

The nod seems to pacify Vlad, and he releases me. His hand immediately goes to the back of his shirt, which he rips over his head in one smooth movement. The sight has me snapping to attention almost immediately.

Unlike the built Vlad I'm used to, identity potion Vlad is... well, a little pudgy. I'm grateful for the distraction from my thoughts and focus on his fat roll to keep myself from falling apart.

"Oh crap, can you grab a bag for my clothes? I will need you to carry them," Vlad states.

His voice breaks through my fog and I nod, only to realize he isn't looking at me. "Err yes, one second."

Pulling out my cellphone I reactivate the "Canada Group" chat. My message is simple: **Under attack. Meet at tree and hurry.**

Fake Marc immediately replies: **Can we help? Already have G/in route.**

I use precious seconds to type back: **No, I don't think so. See you soon.**

Shoving my phone back into my pocket, I rush to the kitchen sink and pray there's a plastic bag underneath like in every other house. I open one of the cabinet doors and sigh in relief. Grabbing the top bag, I gently shut the door and pivot on my heel to face Vlad.

Almost immediately, I wish I hadn't.

His back is arched, his mouth open in a silent scream as his teeth extend and sharpen before my very eyes. A few cracks echo across the kitchen and his legs become disfigured before snapping back into place curled by his sides. The sight is both horrifying and mesmerizing, and like watching a car crash, I can't turn away.

By the time a coat of downy, black fur has covered his newly transformed skin, I feel woozy and unsteady on my feet. I inhale a deep, bracing breath, then gather Vlad's clothes from the kitchen floor and shove them in the plastic bag without making eye contact. I yank Vlad's backpack off mine and shove the bag inside, jamming it on top of the rest of the contents.

A damp, leathery nose bumps my palm while I'm still kneeling on the floor. Raising my eyes from the bag, I connect with a familiar amber gaze staring out of a fur-covered face. Vlad nuzzles further into my hand and whimpers. The sound alleviates some of my overwhelming nausea from watching his transformation. I run my hand down his back, gently scratching his skin with my nails.

This is Vlad, just in a different form than usual.

Another bump of his nose, this time against the small of my back, reminds me of our urgent situation. I rush to the door and unlock the handle, tugging it open just a smidge, as directed.

Pivoting, I find Vlad the wolf right on my heels. He kneels forward, bending his elbows. He rests the front half of his forelegs against the ground. The movement brings his back to a more reasonable height and I clamber atop.

He quickly rises to his full height and I release a surprised squeal, flinging my arms around his neck to stay atop him. My arms overlap each other in a choke hold. I tightly grip his fur as I meld my body against his, hoping my arms are strong enough to keep me from falling off in the woods.

Vlad looks over his shoulder at me and appears to nod approvingly. Then, he nudges the door open with his snout and slips outside.

My eyes screw shut and the wind whips over my body in an angry torrent. My hair flies erratically around Vlad and I, sailing in the air with each bound of his long legs. I wish I'd had the forethought to tie back the long, errant strands, but now that we're in motion, there's no way I'm releasing my grip on his fur for anything.

I can tell by our movement that he's sprinting. His

paws barely touch the ground, pushing against the soft earth of the forest floor in a rapid, repetitive motion of rising and falling, like riding a horse on a merry-go-round.

After a few minutes, I force my eyelids to loosen their tight clench. I may never experience Vlad's shift in this way again. I can't not watch. The second my eyes pop open, I stifle a gasp of surprise. We're much further from Vlad's house than I thought we would be.

I recognize a boulder coming up on the right, and no more than two minutes later, my grandmother's tree appears in our line of sight. My stomach drops to my toes when I see the dirt in front of the tree is empty, meaning my grandmother isn't home.

Vlad skids to a stop, his momentum halting just prior to hitting the bottom step leading into the cottage. He takes a few deep breaths, his sides and chest heaving with each one, jostling me lightly. He is clearly winded from the effort he exerted to get us here as quickly as he did.

The deep, panting breaths eventually steady and Vlad repeats the kneeling motion from before, allowing me to disembark. I slide down his body onto the step. My palms stay against his back and I run my hands down the soft, thick fur. He rumbles, arching into the contact for a brief second, then paces one step away.

He stands to his full height, his head nearly reaching my chin. Nudging me with his nose, he shifts his head to the side. Guessing the meaning of his wordless communication, I remove his backpack and hold it towards him.

Vlad snags the bag between his teeth and slinks into the woods nearby to shift back to his human form. An especially loud crack hits my ears and I cringe slightly. I'm not sure if I'll ever be able to get the image of Vlad shifting into a wolf out of my mind. The process seems much longer and more painful than the transition to human. At least from what I remember when we saw Eric transform in the woods.

I'm distracted from my rogue thoughts when Vlad steps into view from behind a particularly thick, sturdy tree. My gaze scans his human form clad in a white t-shirt and dark jeans. They're fitted to his form like they were painted on, doing nothing to hide his muscular form. He forks his fingers through the longer portion of his messy hair as his amber eyes lock onto mine.

Heat simmers through the connection, and Vlad prowls forward. The only way to describe his expression is predatory. I move closer, transfixed by his lithe grace, even though I'm the prey in this scenario.

The stress of our situation fades with each step closer, until we're standing toe to toe and absolutely nothing else matters. Tipping my head back, I stare up into Vlad's intense eyes. They come closer as he tilts forward, bending over me until his mouth seals to mine.

A contented sigh escapes at the first touch of his

lips. Vlad takes full advantage, sweeping his tongue inside my mouth and deepening the kiss. His palms caress my sides, then grip my hips, yanking them forward, flush against his.

My hands rise to wrap around the back of his neck. I gently play with the short hair at his nape while simultaneously pulling him closer. I want every inch of our skin and mouths sealed against each other until it's impossible to tell where my body ends and his begins.

Vlad ends our kiss with a pained groan. He breaks the grip of my hands while his face retreats. He keeps me tucked against his body with an arm around my waist and rasps, "As much as I want to continue this, I need to ask. Do we have a plan to get in the house? Did your grandma say she was on her way, or do you have a key with you?"

Heat flares across my cheeks as reality comes crashing back. Vlad is too much of a distraction. Between remembering his shift, then being transfixed by his sexy body, my priorities became entirely skewed. My thoughts were so consumed, I forgot we were on the run, and urgently need to get into my grandma's cottage to use her portal.

"Err, I need to call her still," I admit, not making eye contact.

I duck out of Vlad's grip and flip my backpack around my body. My hand shuffles around the items inside until I touch the cool metal side of my phone.

Upon yanking it out, I zip up my bag with one hand, while dialing my grandma with the other.

Anxiety ramps up in my chest with each ring that trills through the phone. My concern grows until my grandmother finally answers on the last ring. Exhaling a sigh of relief, I say, "Grandma? We need to use your portal urgently. Can you come home or do you have a key hidden anywhere?"

"You're in Florence?" She asks, ignoring my questions. "You need to leave, right now." She whispers her words with a frantic urgency that has fear trickling down my spine. "The Coven... they put a bounty out for you. I'm afraid to think of what would happen to you if you were found."

"Okay," I whisper in response. "What about a key though?"

"Ahh, yes Dear. Check underneath the pot to the right of the stairs. I have to go, but I hope everything goes well."

"Thanks grandma."

The only response is the click of the phone as she ends our call. I return my cell to my pocket with a furrowed brow. Then meet Vlad's concerned gaze. "You could hear her?" I ask.

He nods solemnly and intertwines our fingers carefully. He uses the grip to tug me towards the front steps of the cottage. Vlad lifts the planter to reveal a key half stuck in the dirt. He bends over and snags it off the ground at the same time an engine becomes audible in the distance.

I turn to inspect the noise and breathe a sigh of relief. Marc's truck is bumping along the road, closely followed by Vlad's sports car. I snag the key from Vlad's fingertips and rush up the stairs. I'm pushing open the door to the cottage as the vehicles park and doors open.

Alex, Marc, Sylvia, and Leif quickly hop out of the vehicles. As I scan their familiar faces, I realize the effects of the identity potion must have faded, meaning we all look like ourselves once more. The thought hadn't crossed my mind when I was making googly eyes at Vlad two minutes ago, forgetting about his temporary beer gut revealed in his kitchen.

The thought flees as Tony and Greg capture my attention. They emerge from the two vehicles slowly, eyeing our surroundings warily.

One by one, they face the cottage and I grin at the bewildered expressions on their faces. "Welcome to the Spells cottage," I call, extending my arms outwards to encompass the magnificent tree house.

Tony's gaze connects with mine, and he offers a huge grin. "Mira, should've figured you were the one causing all this trouble."

I laugh as Vlad grumbles something under his breath. The rest of the group grabs their gear from the vehicles and bounds across the dirt towards the steps.

After a quick head count, I lift a foot to walk inside the cottage.

A glint of light flashes across the corner of my eye and I twirl back around. Squinting against the glare of the sun, I see a silver sedan bumping down the road in our direction.

"Did your grandma get a new car?" Vlad asks.

16

THE RAT

Vlad

The door to the Silver Volkswagen Beetle opens, but the driver takes their time emerging from the vehicle. A pair of thin, pale legs ending in ankle boots emerges first. The owner of the legs, and presumably the car, leaves them on the ground as a tantalizing glimpse of their identity.

A growl builds in my throat as the urge to shift pulses through my veins in a rage-filled staccato. Those legs definitely do not belong to Mira's grandmother. My wolf can smell trouble in the air, combined with an overwhelming amount of fruity perfume.

The person finally stands, flipping a sheet of chestnut colored hair over her shoulder as she aims a malicious expression in our direction. Unable to contain it any longer, my growl rips free the same second Mira whispers, "Kaylee?"

Kaylee's face widens into a humorless grin, the expression making her appear slightly unhinged. I shove Mira behind me, knowing the previous torment she's suffered at the hands of this girl, and needing to protect her.

Mira's small hand rests against my lower back, and she cranes her neck to peek around my side. I stifle the urge to shove her further behind me, knowing the protectiveness of my wolf can be unreasonable, at times. Right now may be one of those times.

Surprisingly, it's Leif that speaks next. He descends two steps, placing himself in front of the group. "Miss Kaylee, is it?"

I watch as Kaylee's eyes widen slightly in fear. She quickly neutralizes the expression, but she stops edging closer to our group. Her heels dig into the ground, keeping her a few dozen yards away.

"I thought I had already warned you about coming close to Mira," Leif continues, a teasing lilt tinging his words. "Have you come back for more or is there something else I can help you with?"

Kaylee's hands raise to her throat briefly. She shakes her head, slowly lowering her arms and fisting her palms near her sides. Her jaw shifts from side to side and I hear her gritting her teeth, even with the distance separating us.

"I'm here for my boyfriend," she snaps. "And for

Mira. There's a bounty for her and I intend to be the one to turn in the stupid home wrecker."

"Home wrecker?" Mira whispers softly.

Her words must echo as Kaylee responds, "Yeah, why else did you steal my boyfriend in the parking lot outside the Diner... when he was there to meet with me?" She snarks. Her gaze drifts to Leif and her bravado falters briefly as she gulps.

She shakes her head and straightens her shoulders, taking two steps closer. A steady rumble of a growl builds in my throat and I hear Marc behind me mimicking the sound.

Leif descends the final stair, stepping in Kaylee's direction. She shrinks backwards, then glances beseechingly at Greg. "Are you just going to let this psychopath threaten me? I'm your girlfriend and I need your help."

Greg shrugs his shoulders in response, looking a little unsure. I assume that will be his only response. I'm surprised when he also adds, "Just go home Kaylee. We have witching business to handle. I'll be back soon and we can talk about this then."

Her beseeching expression morphs into fury and she spits, "It's too late to 'just go home'. I've already called both of our mothers." She crosses her arms over her chest. "I can't believe you'd side with *them.*" Her eyes scan our group disdainfully.

The blood drains from Mira's face as I watch her in my peripherals. Concern instantly floods through my veins. The feeling morphs into panic as she whispers, "Greg's mom is the Coven Leader."

Her words cause everyone to snap their gaze in her direction, except for Leif. He calmly instructs, "Go on inside. I'll handle this and meet you in there."

I connect my fingers with Mira's and drag her into the house and down the hall. She jogs beside me as we pass through the doorway into the near empty room at the end of the house. The rest of her ragtag group of friends are on our heels, closely followed by Greg and Tony. The urgency of the situation is clear, and no one is messing around.

"Does anyone know how to work this?" I growl, barely containing my wolf as I gesture to the empty doorframe.

Alex nods, and confirms with, "I do."

He rips off the massive backpack he must have acquired in Florence and digs around. His hand reemerges seconds later with a vial of liquid. My gaze wanders over the rest of the group while he completes the necessary steps to activate the potion.

I notice Alex, Sylvia, Tony, and Greg also have on backpacking type packs. It seems everyone but Mira and I used their time in Florence to gather some new gear.

By the time I drag my eyes back to the previously empty doorframe, the shimmery gas that creates the actual portal is near complete. As it touches the last corner, settling into the empty air there, the door to the room flies open.

I brace myself, releasing a vicious snarl. My wolf is on high alert and prepared to protect Mira at any cost. I cease the noise, straightening as I recognize Leif standing in the doorway. Running my eyes over him, he doesn't appear to be injured, only slightly disheveled.

I would never admit it, but my wolf is starting to like the fucker. He's proving to be more trustworthy than I expected. And he may be a dick, but he's just as protective of Mira as I am. My shoulders relax and I offer him a brief nod before giving him my back.

Mira is peering around me once more to check out the rest of the room. Her eyes land on Leif and she asks, "What happened to Kaylee?"

Leif says, "Later."

Then he walks past us through the portal. Not wanting to risk Mira's safety by delaying us any further, I step forward as well. I use my grip to essentially toss Mira through after Leif. She shrieks, but the sound dissipates as she disappears from sight. Feet together, I jump through after.

After sailing through the air, the portal deposits our group in a cluster on the grassy clearing. As I shove my way through random limbs, attempting to free myself enough to stand, I realize we're dangerously close to the edge of the spring's murky water.

A quick skim across the ground fails to reveal a

mass of honey blonde hair, and fear ratchets my pulse into a frenzy. I jump to my feet, disentangling bodies and tossing them to the side in my haste.

"Hey!" Sylvia exclaims, as I pick her up and redeposit her a few feet away.

I ignore her as a painful pulse builds behind my eyes. My fingertips throb, preparing for the claws that are seconds away from tearing free from my skin. I scan the ground again. Once, twice, three times and I can't find her anywhere. My eyes briefly flit to the spring, wondering if maybe...

A throat clears behind me in an irritating manner, clearly meant to garner attention. I pivot on my heel to face the noise, ready to tear out someone's throat.

Leif is standing at the edge of the grass, near the trees, aiming a smirk in my direction. Nestled in his arms is an unharmed Mira. He's holding her bridal style, as if he caught her midair during their fall. Then they peacefully floated the rest of the way to safety, together.

Relief and irritation overtake my panic in equal measures. Shaking my head, I step in Leif's direction as he releases his hold on Mira's feet. He forces her body to slide down his, allowing her feet to plant fully against the ground. Then he relinquishes his grip with another smirk.

Instead of becoming aggravated, I roll my eyes. Leif likes to poke people and hope for a reaction. As much as I hate that he loves my girl, there's no doubt in my mind that Mira is mine.

A screeching voice breaks through the clearing. "Get off my stuff, you *rat*."

I twist around in time to see Sylvia spitting at Greg while he tries to roll off her bag that was mixed into the post-portal chaos. Greg's expression is as furious as Sylvia's tone. His hands clench into fists by his sides, and his cheeks flush with color.

"I'm no rat. I didn't tell Kaylee anything, I just didn't show up to meet her at the Diner. How do we know it wasn't you or Tony, or anyone else in this group that called her?" Greg snaps.

"No one else here is related to the Coven Leader on the NorthWest Coven," Sylvia shrieks.

Greg's furious face sweeps across the clearing, like he can't even stand to look at Sylvia. "This has nothing to do with my mom. Why would I call Kaylee, then hop through the portal anyway? I didn't have to help, but I'm here. I'll leave if someone doesn't fess up to calling Kaylee or the coven. I refuse to be the scapegoat. Hell, I bet it was Tony. I saw him staring at Kaylee like she was a sirloin steak. Dumb mutt."

A cacophony of voices breaks out, coating the area in angry insults and accusations as Tony joins the verbal Spar. Cracking my knuckles, I pace forward intent on smashing the two losers, Tony and Greg, together, which will settle their dispute.

A tiny palm makes a swipe down my arm.

Without looking, I capture Mira's slender fingers in mine. She squeezes my hand lightly in return. Then she drops my fingers and clears her throat expectantly.

None of the dumbasses screaming at each other and jabbing their fingers in the air stop for a single second. Mira shakes her head. "Hey guys, this doesn't seem productive."

Her soft voice floats gently across the clearing but is ignored entirely. Mira tries again, louder this time. "OKAY, I know emotions are high, but this is not the solution."

Exhaling deeply, I bellow, "Enough."

I instantly become the focus of seven livid glares. Despite, or maybe because of, the ire aimed in my direction, my lips flip up into a blasé smirk. Tipping my head towards Mira, I murmur, "Please continue."

She shoots me a grateful smile, tinged with a dose of heat. My wolf hums warmly in response, preening under her attention. I force him to chill out while listening to Mira speak.

"Obviously, our plan didn't work out the way we wanted," she states. Her eyes scan the group, making intentional eye contact with each person gathered in the clearing. "However, tearing each other apart will not help our situation. We're going to have a sixty second silence. If anyone is not committed to being here, to being a part of our legacy mission, I ask that you leave during this time. If anyone has credible information about what happened in Florence, I also ask that you use the silence to say your piece."

The seconds tick by slowly, but no one leaves, and no one speaks. Except for Mira, as she mutters under her breath, "... Twenty Mississippi, twenty-one Mississippi..."

When the minute is up, she nods once. "Okay. I don't think Greg could be the snitch. The witches also ambushed Vlad and I at his house and no one but the original group knew we were there."

Sylvia opens her mouth to respond, but Mira holds her hand up to pause her. "I trust everyone in the original group with my life." She looks pointedly at me, then Leif. "Everyone. We knew we were on borrowed time as soon as we stepped foot in Florence. Despite our precautions, there was a strong likelihood we would get caught."

Mira shrugs, then concludes with, "I'm pretty sure Kaylee followed you and knew we would all be together. Now it's done and over. We made it here and we're safe. We need to focus on getting our camp set-up and figure out our next steps, okay?"

A swell of pride flares in my chest as she finishes her speech. Our entire group nods in response, appreciation clear in their gaze over her words and her leadership. My Little Mir is growing into herself and realizing how strong and capable she is.

17

THE SPRING

Mirabella

I glance around, wondering what to do next. My impromptu speech rallied the troops, but I don't know where to go from here. Thankfully, someone else does.

Leif steps closer to the group lingering near the spring. "We need to set up camp before it gets dark," he instructs, while shucking off his backpack and removing various pieces of camping equipment.

The rest of the group slowly moves towards the scattered backpacks, picking up packs and moving closer to the trees near the edge of the clearing. Vlad quickly leaves my side to join Tony. My gaze lingers on their heads bent together as they have a discussion.

"Crap!" Sylvia exclaims.

My attention quickly flits to her as she struggles to

remove a tent pole from her extra-large backpack. She's seconds away from jabbing herself in the eye when I reach her side. "Can I help?"

She shoots me a relieved grin. "Yes, please do. We just shoved everything into our backpacks, and I can't seem to get anything out now. Plus, setting up a tent solo is super difficult."

Giggling, we create a system. Sylvia holds the bag and I wrestle out the impressive amount of gear jammed inside. Half an hour later, we finally hit the bottom as I heave out another tarp.

Together, Sylvia and I organize the supplies into piles, forming a tent on the ground. After every piece is in the appropriate spot, we have enough left over for at least another half a tent. The sheer volume the backpack contained is astounding.

"First of all, how did so much fit in one pack? And second, why do we have so many extra pieces?" I ask.

Leif's lightly accented voice responds from a short distance behind me, "I spelled it. Same as the rest of the bags."

Twirling around, my eyes skim over Leif's face and slightly skewed blonde hair, to eventually land on his muddy gaze. "Impressive. What are the extra pieces for?"

"An awning." He gestures to the spot he set his tent, a few dozen yards away. Following the line of his arm, I inspect his giant tent preceded by a tarp-covered awning. Underneath are two folding tables holding a cooler, a hot plate, and a few other pieces of gear.

My eyes move further across the clearing, to the next camping spot. Tony and Vlad are standing beside another tent, also equipped with an awning. This one contains a cluster of camping chairs. Two more tents lay further down the row, with Marc, Alex, and Greg milling in and out.

I'm flooded with gratitude as I look around the clearing that is slowly turning into a temporary home for the eight of us. We have no idea how long we'll be out here. As long as it takes, or until we get caught by one of the covens chasing us. Leif seems to have thought of everything we would need, and we're prepared for our potentially lengthy stay.

"Do you need help?" Leif asks, aiming the question at Sylvia and interrupting my observations.

"Err, yes. If you don't mind," she replies sheepishly.

"Why don't you and Mira organize the potions supplies while I finish this up?" Leif suggests as he walks closer and surveys the disarray of camping materials in our area.

I barely refrain from sighing in relief. Pitching a tent is no joke, if the number of tent poles and connectors is any indication. "Thanks Leif. Where are the supplies?" I ask.

"Sylvia or someone in her group has them. They were responsible for potion supplies," Leif says, without looking up from his work on the now half-assembled tent.

"What?" Sylvia asks, sounding horrified.

My gaze lazily drifts away from Leif, in her direction. I fully expect to find her questioning someone's life decisions based on their LifeNovel posts, but her eyes are filled with incredulity and focused entirely on Leif.

"Your group was responsible for all the supplies," she whispers. "We lost time grabbing Marc's truck, and you said you would take care of it."

"No way. We said *if* you didn't have time to message us. You were supposed to stop by your parent's house while we grabbed the camping supplies and spelled the packs," Leif states pointedly. He drops the tent supplies on the ground and crosses his arms as he turns to face Sylvia and I.

"I remember the conversation and that is not what happened," Sylvia fires back, her fists clenching by her side.

My gaze volleys from Leif to Sylvia, then back to Leif again. His mouth cracks as he prepares to retort, but he snaps it shut when I hold a palm in the air. Attempting to calm the panic that is building in my chest, I inhale deeply.

As I exhale, I ask, "Are you saying that neither group gathered potion supplies while we were in Florence?"

"It wasn't one of our tasks, Mira Love," Leif replies.

"It definitely wasn't ours either," Sylvia snaps.

AN UNCOMFORTABLE SILENCE persists from the moment we discovered not a single potion brewing item, other than potion manuals, was included in our camping supplies. The lack of sound mingles with the heavy layer of despair dousing the clearing. As if the weather has adjusted to our mood, a light, hazy mist of rain slowly drifts down from the sky, forcing us to retreat to the awning covered camping chairs.

Somehow in this adventure, I've become a leader of sorts, and I feel as though it's my job to create a plan or at least encourage conversation. Yet, a morose feeling of hopelessness has rooted so deeply in my soul, I can't find the necessary effort to speak. Instead, I watch the rain float to the ground while my thoughts run rampant.

I feel like we've already failed the shifters.

Vlad grabs one of my palms from my lap, twining our fingers together with a gentle squeeze. The silent support does little to boost my mood, but I offer him a feeble smile, anyway.

Sylvia is the only one that holds any lingering optimism about our situation. She continues to blurt random suggestions, despite the group's dour mood. "What if we walk to the nearest city? Maybe we could find supplies there?"

"It's too far to travel by foot," Leif states, shooting her down immediately.

"How do you know?" She quips back. "What if the wolves went? They can cover more distance and they're faster."

"It would take several days at least," Vlad interjects, his voice rumbling with irritation.

As more voices join in to the argument, my brain runs in circles playing the same thought on repeat.

How could we have forgotten the most important supplies for the entire trip?

Instead of sitting around Vlad's house, we should have taken on the task of collecting brewing supplies while the others located the legacies. I ignore the part of my brain that insists we would have no idea how to make a cure, even if we possessed an entire arsenal of potion ingredients and focus on beating myself up. I make the worst leader.

"I think people are approaching," Tony whispers, cocking his head lightly to the side.

The bickering immediately ceases and I glance up sharply, following the direction of his gaze. Two dim beams of light are bobbing and flashing just beyond the line of trees bordering the south side of the clearing.

A chorus of growls emerges from the throats of the shifters. The sound rumbles menacingly across the open space, echoing back and making it sound like we're a group of fifteen wolves, instead of three shifters and five witches.

Two figures emerge from the trees and appear to hesitate slightly. Their concern over the snarling growls ripping through the air is apparent.

"Who are you?" I ask, my voice shaking slightly. I cross the fingers on my free hand, hoping beyond all hopes we haven't been discovered by one of the covens after us.

"Kiddo?" My dad's voice echoes through the area and tears instantly form in my eyes.

I leap out of my chair and rush halfway towards my stilled parents. My steps falter and slow as I remember the last encounter we had. What if they're here on behalf of the coven?

As if she can read my mind, my mom says, "It's just us, sweetie. Your grandma told us where to find you."

The meaning of her words registers to my body first. By the time my brain catches up, I've already resumed my sprint, flying across the damp, grassy ground. I throw an arm around each of my parents, pulling them close as a tear trickles from the corner of my eye. "I've missed you guys."

Since leaving Florence, I haven't allowed myself to dwell on thoughts of my parents or the events of Florence. There was too much else to focus on. Their arrival now, in the middle of one of our most despairing moments, makes me realize how much I've missed their steady, supportive presence.

My mom nods her head, her hair brushing against my cheek. "We missed you too, sweetie."

My dad squeezes us both in tightly, practically crushing the air from my lungs. "But we're here now and that's all that matters."

Eventually I pull away from our embrace and my gaze flits between sets of gray and blue eyes. "What are you doing here? Also, what happened when the coven showed up? Is everything okay? Are you in trouble now too?"

They exchange a lengthy glance. "We think... we think the house is bugged," my mom says.

"Rebecca," my dad chides. "Mira is an adult. She deserves to know. Someone has certainly bugged the house. We've conducted a few experiments and have been able to confirm it. We also assume that they're keeping track of the Morts, and anyone else that's involved with our family at this point. The only thing we aren't certain of is who placed the potion, and why?"

Archibald Golden's name is on the tip of my tongue, but as I mull it over, I become less confident. Esmerelda Fink and Kaylee are both on my potential suspects list and there's no way to rule anyone out at this point. The more I think about it, the more I wonder if the Coven tracked our movements in Florence using this potion.

"I have a few suspicions," I say slowly. "We can talk

that over another time though. Why are you here? I'm happy to see you, but is everything okay?" I ask again.

I cross my arms over my chest, hugging myself as I await their answer. If my parents are also on the run, things must have taken a turn in Florence.

"Everything is fine. We actually can't stay here for long. Molly instructed us to come to the spring while she distracted the coven. She said you and your friends needed a few things and sent us with supplies," my dad replies

Vlad ambles into view as my father finishes speaking. "Arthur, Rebecca," he rumbles.

"Vlad!" My dad exclaims, offering him a one-armed hug like he's a long-lost son. "I'm glad to see you're alright. Can you grab a few of the guys and help me bring things up from the car?"

He nods and jogs away, returning a few seconds later with Marc, Greg, and Tony in tow. "Leif and Alex didn't want to leave you alone up here," he murmurs. He squeezes my fingertips lightly, then walks with my dad and the others to the edge of the tree line and out of sight.

I link arms with my mom, tugging her towards the camp chairs to wait for their return. I fill my mom in about Haven and the Sieves. Then Sylvia asks about her parents. It feels like barely any time has passed before the guys are marching into the clearing laden with two boxes apiece.

I rush over as they stop at the second tent and set them down on our empty tables intended for potion brewing. "What is all this?" I ask.

My mom shrugs, her gaze flirting over the boxes. "It's potions supplies. Your grandma said that you would need it to break the Curse."

18

THE POTION

Mirabella

A steady drizzle of rain leaks from the sky, creating a cadence of pitter patters as it lands against the canvas tarp of the awning. My eyes flash over the supplies, taking inventory for the fifteenth time since my parents left late last night. Love swells in my chest as I look over the ingredients they provided. I can't believe I thought they were aligned with the coven and were the ones that betrayed me.

My eyes hit on a vial filled with a pale blue liquid and an urge to pick it up drives my fingers towards it. Once grasped in my palm, I'm struck with the desire to brew a potion. I pivot around and light the camping burner nestled under the cauldron and scramble for my sketch pad.

Ingredients seem to light within the bottles, indicating they'd like to be added to the potion. I pinch and pour and drizzle each one into the pot, jotting down their names onto the paper as I proceed. Something inside me seems to guide the portions, while the ingredients encourage me to choose them in the pattern they see fit.

After adding three powders, two gases, four liquids, and one piece of root, I scan the vials again, but nothing calls to me. The ingredients portion of the spell feels finished, so I nod once and return to the cauldron.

Staring into the bubbly mass, I grab the stirring spoon. I slowly drift it in a clockwise motion, being sure to scrape all the ingredients off the bottom as I turn, like I'm cooking a stew. I repeat the motion five times, then wait. Watching the liquid swirl to a stop, I glance inside the cauldron, but it doesn't feel complete.

Something urges me to continue stirring, this time moving the spoon counter-clockwise. I repeat the motion three times. As the liquid stops twirling within the inky depths of the cauldron, it emits a low glow. Like a dim flashlight.

Excitedly, I bounce on my toes. I wonder what I brewed. Thoughts race through my mind, competing for attention. What if this is the cure? I need someone with more experience to look over the ingredients, to identify what I've created.

"Guys, guys come see this!" I scream into the clearing, my voice echoing back in an eerie mimic.

My friends slowly emerge from the scattered tents, rushing in my direction. Leif is the first to reach me with his hair sticking in every direction, like he just awoke from a nap.

Vlad is close on his heels, lacking a shirt. Sweat is dripping down his chest, giving the impression I interrupted his work out. His muscles flex with every movement and I find myself quickly distracted by his rippling muscles and stacked abs. I barely notice the rest of the group arriving as I stare.

A throat clearing has me tearing my attention from his glistening body to glance around at my gathered friends. Sylvia appears to be the perpetrator and when my eyes connect with hers, she grins.

"What's up, Mir?" She asks, looking expectantly at my hands like I should be holding something of interest.

"Oh, right," I reply, my cheeks heating. I turn to the cauldron and point at the still-lit contents. "I had this urge to brew. Similar to the way I feel when I need to sketch. For some reason, I feel like this could have something to do with the cure... like it could be the cure."

"You think you just brewed the cure?" Leif asks, his voice tinged with a fair dose of skepticism.

He steps past me to lean his long torso over the edge of the cauldron and inhale deeply. Part of me wants to laugh, it's beyond ridiculous to think he could sniff the contents and identify if it's the cure. But I stifle the urge, as I reconsider the circumstances I'm currently asking the group to believe.

As he straightens, Leif arches an eyebrow in my direction. It serves a dual purpose to communicate his disbelief and prompt my response.

"Yeah... I mean, it could be related to the cure," I trail off, gathering my thoughts. "It felt like the ingredients were influencing me. Like during my witches exams, when I knew which ones to choose despite the inaccurate labels. I don't know how to explain it other than I felt like they were guiding me."

I snag my sketchpad from beside the cauldron and offer it to Leif. The rest of the group has remained silent, watching our exchange. A part of me thinks they're waiting to see if Leif believes me prior to chiming in with their own opinions.

Leif accepts the book and skims his eyes over the page. Vlad peers over his shoulder, glancing at the list of ingredients briefly, then they both turn their gazes to me. Almost as synced as the twins.

"How did you come up with these ingredients?" Leif asks, his eyes probing.

I shrug, "I'm not sure. Like I said... it just felt right."

Leif nods, then peers inside the potion once more. "This is very complex and inedible due to some of the ingredients. Maybe if we poured in on the ground..."

Hope blooms in my chest. Leif is likely the most

experienced witch in our group. If he thinks it will work, it just might work.

"What if we poured it in the Spring?" Marc asks.

I turn to look at him, having forgotten about the rest of our audience. As my eyes pass over Sylvia, Alex, Greg, Tony, then finally reach Marc, I see I have their rapt attention.

A small glimmer of hope shines in Marc's eyes, and I think about the curse through the shifter mindset for the first time. I can't imagine being unable to be angry without shifting or having to worry about losing your humanity if you decide not to shift.

I instantly become more determined than before. If I could access more magic, it would change my life as a witch. But for the shifters? The cure could literally save lives.

"It seems fitting to return the magic to the earth," I say with a nod.

We're all just winging it, coming up with ideas off the cuff. But I'm hoping that together, with our varied experiences and knowledge, we can make this work the way it needs to.

Leif nods and fills a glass vial with my shining potion. It's like the tail end of a firefly in color, astounding and vibrant, blinking lightly as it moves. He silently hands it to me with a soft, encouraging smile.

Inhaling a deep breath, I stride forward, my friends parting to allow me to pass, then following closely on my heels the rest of the way to the spring's edge. I stop when just over a foot separates me from the putrid water, wary of the ground crumbling beneath me.

Squaring my shoulders, I glance behind me and connect with a set of amber eyes. At his reassuring nod, I face forward and chuck the potion as hard as I can. In slow motion, it flies through the air in an arc, aimed towards the water. The descent takes mere milliseconds, but they pass as slowly as possible. The glass hits the water with a splash and a sizzle.

Time speeds up again, but nothing happens.

Water continues to drip from the sky, slowly coating my skin in a slick coat of dampness, and nothing changes. The spring doesn't magically come back to life. I don't suddenly feel more magical. Nothing.

Minutes pass, and my hope wanes. "Maybe it takes some time," I whisper. Then louder, "We probably just need to wait longer."

I hear words from behind me like, "Sure" and "Okay, Mira", but it's clear from the tone that no one else believes the problem is time.

Vlad steps up to my side and intertwines his fingers with mine. "Why don't we go wait under the tarp with the others? I don't want you to get sick."

"I just want to wait here for a few more minutes, just in case. You can join the others though."

"I'll stay awhile if that's okay," he whispers, squeezing my palm tightly.

I glance to his face, curious for a glimpse of his thoughts. His stoic expression is aimed at the lake, though, revealing nothing. So, I turn my gaze the same way, and hold his palm in a death grip as we wordlessly wait.

The sun finally drops below the horizon, leaving us shrouded in darkness. A lantern clicks on behind me and I can hear soft footsteps padding against the ground in my direction. But I refuse to turn, my gaze remaining fixated on the spring, like the second I turn away, I'll miss the cure working.

"Mira," Vlad says softly. "If your potion was the cure, it should have worked by now. It's cold and you're soaked... why don't we get you inside? You can change your clothes and sleep. Tomorrow is a new day. We can try again."

Although his words are gentle, they're also firm. His conviction decimates my last ounce of fortitude. I fill with despair, finally tearing my gaze away from the spring to connect with Vlad's amber gaze.

We stare at each other wordlessly, while I attempt to interpret the emotions in his eyes. I see affection and kindness, but no anger or accusation. Somehow, that gives me the strength I need to stand.

"I thought it would work," I whisper.

Vlad paces forward and gathers me against his chest. I'm grateful for the comfort, but also the shield he provides between me and the rest of my friends. I was so confident, so sure, that this was the cure we had been looking for.

In hindsight, it seems silly. But still it had given me hope. Without it, I feel like I have nothing.

I screw my eyes shut tightly, willing my friends to return to their tents to avoid seeing my breakdown. It's as if an anvil presses against my chest. The weight slowly compresses further downwards, robbing me of the ability to breathe. I'm no longer welcome home. We have no idea how to cure the curse. I'm.... trapped by problems that seem to be unfixable.

Vlad's palm calmly swiping down my back in a soothing motion penetrates my consciousness. Pulling back slightly, I tilt my head back to look at his face. His features are barely visible in the soft glow of the lamp.

"What if we can't find the cure, Vlad? What if I can never return home?"

Vlad leans forward and kisses the tip of my nose, then the corner of my lips. Then he rests his forehead against mine. "We'll find the answers, Little Mir. It might take longer than expected, but I believe in us, you and me. And us, the legacies, here together as a group. You're not alone anymore."

I nod and open my mouth to protest. To say something, but Vlad shushes me softly. "Just turn off your brain for the rest of the night. Let me take care of you and we'll deal with this problem in the morning."

I think over his words and slowly nod against his

chest. His hands find the underside of my elbows and he yanks me forward, melding our bodies together again. I'm still wrapped tightly to his chest when he adds, "And Mira?"

Ignoring my surprise over the use of my full name, I tip my head back again, and meet his intense gaze. "What?"

"Even if we aren't able to return to Florence, we'll find a home. I promise I won't leave you. And I'm pretty confident the others are in it for the long haul too. Anywhere you want to go, I'll follow. For as long as you'll have me."

Tears well in my eyes over his words, and I nod again. Reaching up on my tiptoes, I lay a soft kiss against the bottom of his chin, the furthest point of his face I'm able to reach. Vlad releases a rumbling chuckle and drags my body up his seconds before his lips descend. They connect with mine in a searing, claiming kiss that has the damp cold penetrating my bones quickly fleeing.

I wriggle in his arms, wanting, no needing, our skin to be impossibly closer. Vlad breaks the kiss at that precise moment with a low groan and a whimper emerges from my throat. "We have an audience, Little Mir.'

My cheeks heat as I remember my friends that waited all day in the damp cold, albeit under the tent, to support me and my hopes for my potion being the cure.

Inhaling deeply, I count to ten and then exhale. The air whooshes from my chest, an audible reminder that I'm not actually suffocating under the weight of responsibility. Steeling my spine, I disconnect from Vlad and stride to the awning.

My gaze flits from person to person, scanning faces half seeped in darkness. Their expressions are unreadable, but I can feel their support, strong and steady. Today was a failure, but tomorrow is a new day.

"We'll try again in the morning."

19

THE CURE

Mirabella

I wake early, snuggled against Vlad's chest as tiny rays of sun barely penetrate the clear plastic top of our tent. Every breath brings his pine-ocean scent to my nostrils, and the familiarity causes my muscles to relax. I sink further into our half-deflated air mattress as my thoughts wander.

Maybe I was wrong to think the ingredients were communicating to me. Maybe I just wanted so badly to believe I had all the answers, that I made it all up in my head.

A deep, angsty sigh pushes itself out of my chest. In response, Vlad's arm squeezes my waist, pulling me tighter against him as he nestles his nose into my hair. "What's wrong, Little Mir?" He rumbles against my head, his voice sounding half-asleep.

I wriggle in his hold until he loosens his grip. Twisting around, I keep our bodies close while I crane my head back. My eyes search his face and find Vlad lightly smirking and looking back with one hooded eye. The single amber orb appears more alert than his voice insinuated.

"What are we going to do?" I finally ask, continuing my line of thought from earlier.

"I can think of a few things I'd like to do," he rumbles, wiggling his eyebrows while one eye remains shut.

"I'm serious," I giggle.

"Me too." His words are the only warning I get before he flips me over and settles on top of me. Our mattress lost the majority of its air last night and I can feel the hard ground beneath my spine. The discomfort is quickly forgotten as Vlad gently lifts my hair and peppers my neck with soft, wet kisses.

Desire pools between my legs. I clench my thighs together and arch into him with a breathy sigh. I feel Vlad's smirk against my skin as he pulls the top of my shirt to the side. He continues his descent, laying soft kisses against my collarbone, then the top of my breasts.

The sound of the zipper to our tent unzipping breaks through my lust induced fog and I stiffen. Vlad notices the noise and stops kissing my skin, but remains atop me, a low growl emanating from his chest.

Leif's head pops into the tent, and the tension in my body immediately flees.

"Hey, I'm starting breakfast. Any requests?" He asks, sounding like he's in a very good mood, despite the early hour.

"We're busy," Vlad replies curtly.

"Ahh, my apologies. I would've knocked, but there is no door. Mira, any requests?" Leif asks.

"No, but I'll come help you in a few minutes," I reply with a soft smile.

Vlad growls again, but both Leif and I ignore him. "Thank you, Mira Love."

"Zip the tent on your way out," Vlad rumbles as Leif retreats.

Leif complies with Vlad's request and zips us back inside, but the mood has totally been ruined. Vlad rolls off me, dragging me into his chest with his arm in one fluid movement.

"Bunch of cockblockers," he grumbles under his breath and I can't help but laugh in response.

"I'm going to change and help Leif," I state, trying to unravel the tight grip of Vlad's arms. Every time I get one off me, it seems like five more grow back in its place, gripping me tightly to Vlad's warm chest. "C'mon let me go," I finally say, out of breath and giggling.

"Fine," he agrees reluctantly, laying back against the bed, placing his palms beneath his head on the pillow.

The second I leave our sleeping bags zipped together, I shiver. I didn't realize how much Vlad's body heat was acting as a heater until I was no longer attached to it. I rush to my backpack and grab a sweatshirt and socks, quickly dressing to ward off the chill.

Blowing a kiss to Vlad, I flit out of the tent before he has a chance to grab me again. Wandering over to Leif's camp spot, which hosts our kitchen set up, my eyes roam over the clearing and the spring, hoping to see any possible sign my concoction worked. As far as I can see nothing differs from yesterday, despite the potion I dumped into the murky acidic water.

A frustrated sigh forces itself out of my throat as I join Leif. He turns to me, concern peppering his expression while he holds a spatula in the air. "Is everything okay, Mira Love?"

"Yeah..."

But it isn't. My paintings brought us to this clearing, but what I've failed to tell the group is long before we started searching for the legacies, I painted our failure in vivid detail. I'm growing more concerned with each passing day that the painting is accurate.

Glancing up, I see Leif has returned to face the hot plate, flipping pancakes and humming. "Do you think everything I paint is an accurate prediction of the future? Or is there a chance it could be wrong?"

Leif stops humming but doesn't turn back around. He taps the edge of the spatula against the griddle a few times. My mouth cracks, preparing to repeat the question, unsure if he heard me the first time. He speaks before I form the words. "The sight has been known to be a volatile type of magic. From the little I know; the present has the ability to drastically affect the future. Therefore, if something is predicted, but actions and intentions shift, different paths are taken. Because of that, predictions may not come true."

I contemplate his words, feeling slightly reassured. "Good to know," I whisper. Hoping against all odds he's right.

AFTER BREAKFAST, the urge to create strikes like lightning. Vlad leaves with Marc and Tony for a run in the mountains, so I have the tent to myself. Pulling out a sketch pad, I lose myself in the soothing motion of scratching a pencil across the paper.

An image shaded in charcoal and gray quickly forms. But I'm not ready to stop yet. Flipping the page without discerning my drawing, I create another image, etching it out on the paper slowly.

The act is soothing, the sound calming, with each scrape becoming a part of an image, but also relieving my tension. Despite all the recent stress and failure, I find my lips forming into a cheerful grin. Creating, especially painting, has always been my happy place.

Now, through quiet time in my tent, I allow my fingers to wander freely. Instead of forcing myself to think about the shifters or the curse, or how every image I draw should help move us forward, I empty my mind and just sketch.

Hours pass as I lose myself in detailed renderings, creating at least a dozen. I don't allow myself to check them, I just keep drawing. I don't stop until the zipper from the tent begins to move, breaking my focus.

Expecting Vlad, I lounge back on the semi-deflated air mattress, attempting to strike a seductive, yet casual pose. A flash of violet pops into view, then Sylvia pounces on the bed beside me. "Hey Mir. You've been hiding out all day. What are you up to?"

"Just sketching," I say with a laugh as I sit upright.

"Do you mind if I join?" She asks, already withdrawing her phone from her pocket.

"Not at all."

I smile as she pulls up her LifeNovel despite the insanely slow cell signal around here. She scrolls through, and begins huffing as she reads posts, muttering under her breath. It's much more tame than usual, and I eye her curiously. But her gaze doesn't lift from her phone.

After a few seconds, I turn back to my sketch pad. Flipping to the next empty page, I place the tip of my charcoal pencil against the paper. I complete a single swipe before the noise of the tent zipper punctuates the silence, again.

Expecting Vlad again, I place my sketching materials on my lap and fluff out my hair a little. Sliding my eyes to the side, I see Sylvia is still focused on her phone. When I look back to the entrance of the tent, I find a set of emerald eyes staring back at me.

"Mira... and Sylvia. What are you two up to?" Alex asks, stepping inside and sealing the tent shut behind him.

"Just uh, hanging out," I reply, slightly curious why my tent is suddenly becoming full.

"Cool, cool. Do you mind if I join you? I brought a book."

"Sure, why not?" I reply with a small smile.

As my gaze returns to the pad, the zipper unzips again. This time I don't bother to look up. As strange as it sounds, this time I can tell from the speed of the zipper it isn't Vlad. "Yes, come in. Yes, you can stay."

From my peripherals, I spot Leif. He slinks inside with a smirk and settles on the edge of the bed beside me. He shuffles a deck of cards between his fingers, but doesn't make a move to play with them. Instead, he keeps twisting his head to the side, eyeing the mostly blank page of paper held between my hands.

I open my mouth to reprimand him and tell him to keep his eyes to himself. I can't create if I know I'm being watched relentlessly. But wouldn't you know it, I'm interrupted by the zipper again before I can form the words.

This time Greg pops his head in. "Hey Mira, have you seen any of the..."

"We're all in here," I state dryly, gesturing around

the tent. "And the shifters are on a run. You're welcome to join us, if you'd like."

Greg nods, stepping inside and zipping the tent closed to keep the rain and bugs outside. He settles onto the edge of the air mattress and begins twiddling his fingers, looking agitated. Every move he makes I see out of the corner of my eye, distracting me from my creative process.

I try to focus on my sketch pad again, but eventually give up. There's too much anxious energy in my now overcrowded tent. The second I flip my sketch pad closed, Leif suggests, "Gin Rummy?"

Despite the looming threat of the covens closing in on us, and the unsolved mystery of the curse, I find myself shrugging. "Sure, why not?"

20

THE THROWDOWN

Mirabella

For the first time since I've started sleeping in the same bed as Vlad, I sleep restlessly. My eyes pop open at the slightest sound and my brain works on overdrive, playing with ideas on how to solve the curse.

Yesterday, we didn't make much progress, spending most of the evening in my tent playing games. It was a nice distraction, but now the fear that we won't be able to find a cure in time is looming.

When sunlight eventually seeps into the tent, I free myself from Vlad's arms despite his grumbling protests and get dressed. Gathering my drawings, I walk straight to the tarp holding our food and wait for the rest of the group to arrive.

A few minutes later, a sleep crusted, but no less

handsome Vlad joins me. He opens the cooler and piles food on the table next to the skillet while it heats. Leif is next to join us, looking peppy despite the early hour, and that's when I remember his time zone is three hours ahead. Despite it feeling early to us, this is probably mid-morning to Leif, if he were at home.

Pushing aside the thought, I focus on the booklet in front of me. I didn't look at my sketches last night, giving up on drawing as my tent slowly filled. Now, as the guys cook breakfast, I flip through my sketch pad with a furrowed brow. The images all appear to be similar, each with a person standing in front of a bubbling cauldron.

Growing frustrated, I rip the pages from my sketchpad and lay them across the counter in a row. My gaze skims over them, attempting to discern some type of pattern, or if they're important at all. I'm so engrossed in the task, I don't realize the others have slowly trickled into our make-shift kitchen to join in on breakfast.

"Is this each of us brewing a potion together?" A soft voice asks from above my left shoulder.

My head whips up from the paper and I almost smack my shoulder against Greg's too close nose. "What?"

He hesitantly points to the images, a slightly fearful look present in his gaze. Maybe I look deranged, or maybe it's due to the close call with his nose. "These look like we're all taking turns brewing a potion together. The cauldron looks in the same state in each image, the only difference is, some of us are stirring in the opposite direction as others."

"How do you know that?" I whisper.

"Well... your pictures are pretty detailed. You can see in these five," he points to five of the sketches laying across the table. "The potion is twirling in one direction. And in these three," he points to the remaining images. "The potion is swirling in the opposite direction."

I nod in acceptance, but not understanding. My gaze immediately focuses on the images for closer inspection, wanting to see what Greg does. I slowly notice what he's saying and an idea blossoms in my head. I snatch up my sketchbook, flipping back to the page where I wrote the instructions for the potion I brewed two days ago.

My eyes skim the page three times. Then, I glance up, my gaze flitting across each person standing under the tarp as the smell of pancakes and sickly, sweet syrup drifts into my nostrils. "I know what we need to do. We need to brew the potion, together in order for the cure to work."

Silence fills the space for point five seconds before everyone speaks at once. My eyes widen at the cacophony of voices, quickly overwhelming me.

"How do you know—"

"Why would we—"

"Who would—"

"Enough," Leif roars.

Everyone in the group falls silent, allowing me the opportunity to explain. I send Leif a grateful smile prior to speaking. "Okay. From my sketches it looks like we all need to complete a specific step while creating the cure."

"Even the wolves? I've never brewed a potion before," Tony interjects, taking a step backwards as if he isn't comfortable with the idea.

"Yeah, even the wolves," I reply. Turning to face Leif, figuring he's the most knowledgeable, I ask, "Would anything negative happen to the shifters if they took part in brewing a potion?"

"Well, it seems like there's only way to find out, Mira Love."

"Are you sure this will work?" Sylvia asks nervously for the twelfth time.

"Yes, I'm sure. Look at the sketches," I reply without glancing up.

I slowly add the last ingredient, a small bit of dogwood bark, then I inhale deeply. My gaze remains fixated on the potion, watching as it transforms from a murky, bubbling liquid to a shining bubbly liquid. Just like before.

"Okay, we each need to stir one full revolution," I instruct, glancing around the group gathered behind me. A collection of apprehensive faces stare back at me attentively, soaking up each word.

Tony, Marc, and Vlad seem particularly nervous, so I take the time to add on to my explanation and reiterate what I told the group earlier. "Witches need to stir one time, one full revolution, clockwise. Shifters need to stir one time, also one full revolution, but counterclockwise. Wait until the liquid has finished swirling before changing directions and make sure you scrape the ingredients off the bottom."

I connect with each gaze in the group, waiting for a nod of affirmation and understanding. Once everyone has signified, they know what to do, I twirl around and face the cauldron. Inhaling deeply, I cross my fingers, hoping this works.

I grab the ladle and stir one full, clockwise revolution. Nothing in the potion changes, but I step away, allowing Sylvia to take my place. She completes her circle, and the group continues under my watchful gaze, each witch taking their turn.

Marc is the first shifter to step up to the cauldron. His tentative gaze meets mine. "Are you sure about this? I've never touched a potion before."

I smile reassuringly. "I'm as sure as I can be. If it doesn't work, we'll just have to try something else."

He nods, his chest heaving as he grabs the ladle and completes one quick, full revolution. Tony seems more confident as he steps forth. Then, it's finally

Vlad's turn. He kisses my cheek as he moves forward, then grabs the spoon and stirs the potion a single time.

The second the liquid stops moving, the shine instantly dims and the color transitions to an inky black. It instantly absorbs all the light, and hope, from the clearing.

"Is it supposed to do that?" Leif asks.

"I have no idea," I respond. "Should we dump it into the spring and see if it does anything?"

Silence greets my question. Vlad finally replies, "It can't hurt anything, right?"

I nod, despite my previous confidence waning. I'm unsure if it will help at this point, but I'm hoping it won't make things worse. Maybe it was a mistake to have the shifters touch magic?

I thought there would be nothing worse than nothing happening, but the longer I look at the deep, onyx colored potion, the more concerned I become that the shifters may be in danger if we use the potion we created.

Turning to Leif, I eye him beseechingly, hoping he has the answer, but he shrugs lightly. He steps forward and squeezes my palm gently. "I think it will be okay, Mira Love. We have nothing to lose."

Despite the fear bubbling up my throat, I nod and ladle the potion into a vial. With a deep breath, I square my shoulders and walk in the direction of the spring. The rest of the group trails after me, but I hardly pay them any mind. I'm too busy taming my errant thoughts, attempting to focus on hope instead of fear.

"Stop." The command echoes through the spring and isn't a voice I recognize.

Glancing up from the ground, my eyes catch on a group of witches wearing black robes. A gasp tears from my throat, my hand belatedly reaching for my mouth to silence it. In my peripherals, I see our entire group turning to face the coven witches. The boys appear to square off their shoulders as if they're preparing for a fight.

Vlad inches closer, closing the distance of three steps that remained between us, practically blocking me from view.

"What do we do now?" Alex mutters through a tense jaw, waiting for instructions.

Apparently, his voice easily carries across the clearing, as one of the witches responds, "You hand over the potion and give yourselves up."

An image flashes through my mind. One I haven't seen, but have painted in vivid detail. It's my body laying broken across the ground at the spring, laying in a pool of blood. I shake my head to clear it and make a split-second decision. This fight can't happen without destroying us all.

One of the witches whips a bottle from her robes. Before she has a chance to use it, I dash forward and press a soft kiss against Vlad's lips. "I love you," I whisper. Then I leap.

My legs push against the ground, carrying my small body over the crumbling, grassy ledge and into the spring. I tilt the bottle to the side while I'm still mid-air allowing the liquid to pour into the water. Time stills as it trickles downwards, reaching to the ground slowly, and hitting the acidic spring seconds before I do.

I screw my eyes shut as my feet splash through the surface. Inhaling a last deep breath, I brace myself, expecting the pain of being eaten alive by the toxic water. Instead, I'm sucked into the liquid like entering quick sand. Then I'm suspended.

The very texture of the water seems to change as I linger there. Then the ground begins to shake, in pulsing waves like a magnitude eleven earthquake has suddenly triggered, splitting the very core of the earth in two. The vicious movement jostles me as I remain suspended in the substance that feels more like Jell-O than acid.

Just as my lungs start to scream from a lack of air, the water pushes me upwards, like a geyser. I'm shoved from the depths, up to the surface and spit onto the grass in the direct center of the feuding groups.

The second after I emerge from the water, Vlad rushes towards me. I can barely focus on him as I turn over to my belly and gag, spitting up water that I must have inhaled during my time under the surface. By the time I stop, my throat is raw and my eyes water, but I'm grateful that I'm still alive.

The coven witches cackle as a unit, the sound terrifying and ominous as it coats the clearing. Glancing around, I realize nothing appears to have changed, which is probably what triggered their mirth.

My observations are confirmed when a middle-aged woman with auburn hair steps forward, placing herself at the front of the coven witches. Her reedy voice echoes across the clearing as she hurls words at us like daggers. "*You*, a group of newly licensed teenage witches with a couple of dogs in tow, thought you could break a centuries old curse?" She pauses to cackle, bending in half as if our actions are too hilarious to contain her laughter while standing upright.

When she finally regains control, she continues, "All your little experiment did was cause the earth to shake. Now quit playing games and surrender. Return to the coven with us peacefully or you will not like the consequences."

My entire body wilts in disappointment over our failure. I was confident my drawings contained the answer, and the potion we brewed would be the cure. But we failed, and now it's too late.

I gather all my strength and use it to drag my body partially upright. Resting on my hands and knees, I inhale deeply in preparation of pushing my weary body to its feet. As my palms push against the earth, the ground rumbles again, knocking me against the grass once more.

The movement continues, and the trees and mountains surrounding us snap and crackle ominously. Then as quickly as it started, the sound stops. I hold my breath, keeping my body still as I pray these earthquakes are a sign the potion worked.

Then something magnificent happens. My hands and arms begin to tingle with a light, tickling sensation. A slight glow emanates from my palms and I gasp.

Tearing my gaze away from my arms, my eyes skim across the clearing. Every witch and shifter present is glowing, emitting a bright orange or yellow light. An intense feeling flashes through my limbs and as quickly as it began, the glowing light blinks out.

I return to my hands and knees, preparing to heave myself to my feet, but my previously aching and exhausted body feels reinvigorated. I easily rise to my feet in time to see the previously murky lake water transition to a clean, clear spring in a single wave. The crystal blue water glints in the sun, flashing into my eyes as I gasp in surprise.

"We did it."

"Mira, we did it," Sylvia squeals.

She launches herself at me, nearly toppling us both into the water before I catch my footing. I return her grip, squeezing her tightly as disbelief and joy war in my mind.

Did we actually do it?

Seconds into our embrace, I remember the coven witches. I instantly release Sylvia, preparing to defend us against an imminent attack. Although we won, I can't imagine the coven conceding that easily.

To my surprise, the coven witches exchanges glances, then slowly trickle from the clearing, until only the auburn haired witch remains. She stands stock still as she stares at the spring, confounded. As if she can feel our eight pairs of eyes watching her, she finally glances up then moves her gaze around the clearing.

She glares and opens her mouth to speak, then quickly snaps it shut. It appears she isn't as bold without her backup. Twirling on her heel, she retreats in a wave of billowing robes, dashing towards the trees to follow the rest of the coven.

I watch her until she disappears from sight. Then, I continue looking, still not believing that this is the end after such a lengthy journey.

It seems almost... too easy.

"What do we do now?" Sylvia asks, her whispered words breaking the silence of the clearing.

I tear my gaze away from the trees to glance at her, then the rest of the legacies standing around me in a semicircle.

"Now, we learn to use the rest of our magic."

21

THE IDEA

Vlad

"I still can't believe it's all over," Mira murmurs. She focuses her gaze on the canvas ceiling of our tent, while we lay side-by-side.

I lean over and press a gentle kiss against her forehead, and whisper, "I still can't believe how incredible you are."

She giggles in a way that says she doesn't believe me. Instead of trying to convince her with words, I recline back on the half-deflated air mattress and pull her into my chest. Mira nestles into my side without protest, releasing a contented sigh. It lasts for about seven seconds before she begins wriggling.

Chuckling, I loosen my grip and Mira moves to straddle me. I lay back further, allowing her to take the reins. She does so gladly, aligning our still clothed centers, then leaning forward to press a soft kiss against the corner of my mouth.

My tongue darts out, sliding against her lower lip until she relents, sealing her mouth against mine. Without prompting, my hand tangles into her hair, pulling her face closer to mine as I claim her.

By the time we separate, we're both panting. Mira touches her fingers to her lips briefly, looking deep in thought. But before I can ask about it, she rips off her shirt, closely followed by her bra. Once her upper half is completely naked, she boldly meets my eye and offers a saucy wink, closely followed by a giggle.

My eyes leave her face to skim her body, my hands tracing a path down her sides to rest on her hips as I lean forward to seal our lips together. Before they connect Mira asks in a breathy voice, "Are you planning to keep your clothes on?"

I peck her lips, then yank my shirt off. Barely breaking eye contact with the grey-eyed girl that owns me, I throw it to the corner of the tent. Then, my hands return to her waist. "Better?"

She nods, grinning in my direction as she tips forward to trail her fingertips over my stomach. My muscles clench in her wake as she explores every defined ridge of my abdomen. Mira moves her face closer to my body, sliding her mouth across my skin in hot, open-mouthed kisses.

I groan as her tongue flits out and grazes my nipple. My patience starts to wear thin and I snag the back of her elbows to push her upright. "Let me take care of you," I murmur.

My fingers slide to the button of her jeans at the same time hers do. In a clash of hands and limbs we ungracefully shed our last vestiges of clothing. Mira returns to my lap, her naked body perched on mine, and I can't think of a single view that I would enjoy more.

Her nipples point at attention, and I slide my hand upwards to caress the sensitive buds. Rolling them between two fingers causes her to moan, loudly. I try to sit upright, seeking another kiss, but she pushes a palm into my chest, urging me to lie back.

She tentatively wraps a hand around my cock, sliding the firm skin up and down between her palm. I groan and thrust upward into her hand, enjoying the sensations she's building with her tiny palms.

Licking my thumb, I slide a hand down her body and connect with her clit. I swipe against it twice before she pushes me away to line my cock up to her pussy instead. She slides down slowly, inch by torturous inch of her slick heat covering me.

My hooded gaze follows her every movement as she tests out the position. She slowly slides up and down, extending the delicate torture further. I clench my fists, allowing her to be in control, until I can't stand it any longer.

Leaning forward, I connect our lips once more and flip her over in one smooth movement. She releases a surprised gasp, which I quickly swallow, devouring the sound as I lick and nip at her mouth.

Resting against my forearms, I place a palm beneath her head, worried about the hard ground beneath our mostly deflated bed. Then I set the pace, thrusting deeply enough to drag a groan from my throat.

I use my other hand to angle her bottom upwards, thrusting again. The angle causes Mira to release another gasp and I smirk against her lips. Finding her sweet spot, I continue sliding in and out at a punishing pace.

Her legs tremble as she creates a steady sound of mewling cries, and I pull back slightly, watching her face as her orgasm tears through her. The sensation of her body clenching around mine has me falling over the edge right after her with a guttural groan.

I place my forehead against Mira's and wait for our breaths to steady, then withdrawal, tugging her back against my front. I lazily trace a design on the skin of her belly with my fingers and she releases a contented sigh. After a pause she asks, "What do we do now?"

"Round two? Dinner?" I suggest throwing out ideas.

Mira giggles and runs her hand down my arm in a soothing swipe. "No. I mean next in life. It doesn't feel like we can return to Florence after this. Even though the curse has been broken... I don't really trust the coven. Or the council, for that matter." She pauses, her fingers tapping against my arm.

I remain silent, stilling my hand to allow her time to think through all the ideas pinging around in her brain. She finally continues, "Florence is where I was raised, but it just doesn't feel like home. Not anymore."

Mira releases a wistful sigh and I place my fingers underneath her chin, tipping her head so our gazes can lock. "Little Mir, I love you."

She gasps, her hand flying to her mouth as her eyes widen in shock. "I love you too," she exhales past her hand in a quiet whisper.

Her surprise over my feelings has a soft grin forming across my face. Mira has no idea the effect she has on people. Shaking my head, I murmur, "Like I said before, I will follow you anywhere you want to go. I'll do that for as long as you wish. Wherever you go, I go."

I seal my words with a kiss. A brand created by the tangling of our tongues, teeth, and lips, leaving no room for question that she is mine, and I am hers. My words are a vow that I will adhere to, for as long as she'll let me.

When we break apart, Mira looks at me adoringly. Her voice is surprisingly firm as she repeats, "Where you go, I go." After punctuating the statement with the nod, she rolls off the air mattress and begins tugging on her clothes in a haphazard manner.

"Where are you going?" I ask.

"To gather the others. I have a plan."

At a slightly slower speed, I gather my clothing and redress. By the time I exit, I see Mira dashing across the far end of the clearing, unzipping the second to last tent, then scampering to the last tent in the row.

She collects all the legacies, herding us to circle under the breakfast tent. Leif pulls out food to cook breakfast, as I eagerly await hearing her plan. A wide grin splits Mira's face as she scans our group. Everyone looks groggy and exhausted, but their attention is fully focused on Mira, at the head of our wonky, misshapen circle.

"Vlad and I were talking," she begins, shooting me a soft, sweet smile before her gaze pings around the group. "And it doesn't feel right to return to Florence. At least not for us. To be frank, I can't think of anywhere it seems right to return to or go to next."

She pauses, twisting her torso to glance at the spring of crystal-clear water behind her. The blue depths sparkle lightly in the sun, inviting us inside for a swim to cool off in the quickly heating, summer day.

"I think what feels right is to stay here." Mira opens her arms wide to encompass the clearing surrounding us and the lake.

My brow furrows as I contemplate her words. Is Mira wanting to build something like her grandmother's cottage?

"Err, you want to live in a tent or like a tree or

something now?" Sylvia asks, puckering her lips in distaste following the question.

Good question, Sylvia.

Expectant gazes return to Mira, and she releases a soft giggle and shakes her head. "No way. I want us," she circles the group with her hand then continues, "To form an Alliance and build our base here. To protect the spring and to protect our magic."

"What would this *Alliance* look like?" Leif asks, muttering the word Alliance like someone just asked him to eat dog shit.

"Basically, just like this," Mira states with a shrug. "It would be a group of witches and shifters working together to protect their respective magic, this spring, our heritage, and to teach other's what we've learned. Instead of belonging to a coven or a council, we would belong to the Alliance."

She releases a wistful sigh. "We have so much strength here. Marc, Vlad, and Tony, you could teach the wolves about shifting, speed, and control. Along with anything else, young shifters may need to know."

"Sylvia, Leif, Alex, Greg and I can teach potions, the sight, and once we learn more about it, spell casting. But most of all, everyone here can teach about acceptance. Witches and Shifters don't have to live together or cross-breed or anything like that if they don't want to. But they shouldn't be pushing each other to the brink of extinction either."

"How would we support this Alliance?" Alex asks.

Seconds after Marc adds, "Would we have to leave everything else behind to join?"

My thoughts immediately jump to the Daily. Mira probably has no idea how truly passionate Marc is about the news. Although Alex kept up the appearances of being Marc, he clearly doesn't have the same passion for the paper. Marc has dreamed of owning a newspaper his entire life, and I'm not sure he would give up his dream for some half-baked plan to start our own city.

Mira seems to have a similar thought. "I would love for the Alliance Compound to be everyone's full-time residence, but if you aren't interested, I understand. Or if you want to come here on holidays or a few weeks a year, I also understand. I want to share this dream with all of you because we've been through so much together, but if its only my dream... I understand."

"As far as sustainability, I have a few ideas. I was thinking we could grow most of our own food. It might be difficult to receive supplies up here anyway, but I also was playing around with the idea of starting our own online Newspaper. We could call it the Magic Times and cover anything big that's happening anywhere in the world, in our community."

"The Magic Times," Marc murmurs, rolling the words around in his mouth, trying it out for size.

Mira nods excitedly, "We could take turns travelling to cover events and recruit more people to join the Alliance. We could offer our services to covens and shifters to help solve mysteries or help mend relationships. I'm literally bursting with ideas. I can't wait to get started."

"I'm in," I state, breaking a growing silence, with six people looking contemplative.

"Me too," chimes Sylvia. "I want to be part of the Alliance mystery solving team." She does a crazy high kick following her words, almost taking out Tony. He dodges at the last second and Sylvia doesn't appear to notice.

Once both feet are solidly on the ground, she extends a hand into the center of the circle, like we're a sports team about to call out a cheer. Shaking my head, I step closer and place mine atop hers.

"Mira Love, I can't think of anything I'd like more than to start an Alliance with you," Leif replies, adding his hand atop mine and Sylvia's as I emit a small, territorial snarl.

Marc and Alex exchange a glance and Alex adds, "We're in." Two more hands join the stack in the center.

Expectant gazes shift to Greg and Tony, and I wonder what they're thinking. Out of everyone here, they're likely the least invested. They just got sucked into this adventure mere days ago and really have experienced little of our group dynamic.

"What the hell, I'm in," Tony exclaims, slapping his hand atop the twins,

Greg looks like a deer caught in the headlights as he slowly shakes his head. "I'm sorry, guys. I know you've been through a lot, but my life path is already set for me. I'm expected to take over the Northwestern Coven. I've been training for it since I learned about magic, and if I left, I don't know who would take over." He shrugs and slowly backs out of the circle. "I'll be sure to spread the word for you guys though. And you know you have a friend in Florence if you ever need anything."

Mira nods and waves goodbye as Greg retreats to his tent, presumably to grab his things and bail. I never really liked that guy much anyway. He's always been spineless, letting Kaylee boss him around and standing witness as she fucked with Mira. Good riddance.

My gaze returns to Mira as she shrugs and states, "Well, six out of seven ain't bad."

Leif grumbles, "Can you get in here and get on with this so we can all stop holding hands?"

I stifle a laugh at the grumpy, facetious asshole as Mira steps into the circle. She places her hand on top of ours and bounces it one, two, three times. Then she lifts it into the air and yells, "To the Alliance."

An awkward, off sync echoing of her words follows from the rest of us.

"Well, we'll work on that," she says with a giggle.

Then the seconds tick by as we glance at each other, wondering what to do next.

"Uh, so what now?" Sylvia finally asks after at least ten minutes of standing there, the echoes of our voices long since faded.

Mira smirks, a beauteous expression I've never seen grace her face before. Then, she says, "We get to work."

EPILOGUE
THE ENDING(ISH)

Mirabella
Twelve Months Later

Kicking off my shoes, I allow my toes to sink into the grass as I stand side-by-side with Sylvia. Together we watch Vlad, Marc, and Tony wrestle a sectional sofa through the doorway of the main building to our new compound. They're stuck in the doorjamb with Vlad resting the piece of sofa against his knee while he aggressively jabs a hand in the air, communicating some message to the other two guys.

"I'm so happy we get to move out of the trailers and into the house today," Sylvia states, her gaze fixated on the guys as they struggle.

"Mhmm," I respond. Her words barely register as I watch the scene unfold before us.

"Do you think we should help them?" Sylvia asks. Her gaze is focused on the guys with a single hand raised, already poised to cast a spell.

"Nah, they'll figure it out eventually, right? Plus, it's kind of fun to watch," I reply, eyeing Vlad's shirtless torso as it flexes and ripples in time to his movements, lifting the couch from his knee. Then, I discreetly probe the sides of my mouth with my fingertips, checking for any stray drool.

Glancing at Sylvia, I catch the tail end of her eye roll. I swat a hand at her, but she ducks out of the way quickly to avoid the blow. "You're being kind of evil, right now," she exclaims in mock offense.

This time, I roll my eyes. Releasing a sigh, I state, "Fine, you can help."

A huge grin splits Sylvia's face as she lifts her hand in the air. She slowly pinches two fingers together, then uses them to pivot the couch ever so lightly. The new position allows the guys to effortlessly slide the slightly too-large piece of furniture through the doorframe with ease.

"Show off," I mutter.

Sylvia giggles in response, then strides away, presumably to help the guys move in the rest of our new furniture, faster. She's really taken to spell casting, much more quickly than I have.

A few months ago, the Sieves brought us some

vague, philosophical books about spell casting, and we learned most of magic is about intention. There aren't any other rule books, or spell books out there for us to study, not anymore. They were destroyed long ago, when witches lost their magic, forcing us to learn primarily from trial and error.

It's easiest for me to cast a spell if I can see the object, but I'm the least advanced in our group. This morning when we practiced, Leif was able to procure breakfast for us, which he definitely could not see. And Sylvia is excellent at manipulating objects... and I'm still trying to overcome the error portion of trial and error.

Maybe I don't possess the innate ability, or maybe I've been focusing too much of my effort on attuning the sight. Supposedly, my mothers' side of the family had an affinity for the sight back in the day. At least according to my grandmother. Ultimately, I'm hoping to channel that, which is taking up most of my free time. It's my goal to be able to predict the future without drawing or sketching eventually, but at present, I'm working on accuracy.

Vlad appears in the doorway, interrupting my thoughts as his sheen of sweat glints lightly in the sun. "Are you sure we have to do this all by hand?" He asks. His rumbly voice drifts across the clearing, sounding only mildly annoyed. Even with the distance separating us, I can feel his heated gaze skimming down my body as he awaits my reply.

"Err, yes," I baldly lie, eyeing his torso. "Our spell casting isn't that great yet. There's really nothing we could do to help."

Vlad nods in response, then turns back to face the truck.

My spell casting definitely is not up to snuff, but Sylvia and Leif probably could offer assistance of the magical variety. Thankfully, the former is willing to be complicit in my lie and the latter is running an errand. My gratitude ramps up even further, as Vlad's muscular back flexes with the effort to pick up a stack of boxes and stride towards the house.

My eyes follow him until he's out of sight, then greedily linger in the doorway, hoping he'll reappear. After a few moments, I reluctantly drag my eyes away from the porch, admiring the enormous structure we've built from the ground up.

Originally, the intention was to build the Alliance compound directly beside the spring. Due to various concerns, we eventually decided on a clearing just under a mile away. It allows easier access for vehicles and more privacy, making it a better location.

The columned wrap-around is the preface for a house covered in pale gray siding with navy shuttered windows. A few smaller structures pepper the ground behind the main home, but they barely register in my gaze.

I continue moving my eyes away from the building and catch on a vehicle pulling up into our large circular drive. The emblem of a catering company is noticeable on the side and I hustle over to greet them. The Alliance's Grand opening is still a month away, but in less than twenty-four hours, the rest of our close family and friends are arriving for their first look of the completed cluster of buildings.

LATER THAT EVENING, my nerves ramp up. Anxiety and excitement combine to thrum through my veins as I stand on the porch waiting for the boys to allow me inside. After the moving trucks were emptied, I was barred from the house to "give them space to set up".

Finally, the door cracks, revealing a sliver of Vlad's face. "Are you ready, Little Mir?" he asks with a smirk.

Fighting the urge to huff, I nod once. My patience is wearing thin and I am seriously questioning the guy's ability to decorate without my help. Vlad chuckles at my annoyance and slips through the door and onto the porch without allowing me a glimpse of the interior.

He takes two long strides, then sweeps me into his arms to cradle me against his chest. I squeal in response, swatting at Vlad's shoulder. He chuckles instead of dropping me and carries me over the threshold like a new bride.

My irritation morphs into awe within seconds. I barely register my feet tapping against the ground as Vlad releases me and my jaw drops to the floor.

As a group, we picked out the large pieces of furniture. Meshing Leif's cabin style with the twin's farmhouse feel, and mine and Sylvia's eclectic taste in décor. My eyes skim over the bulky furniture scattered through the main rooms, but that isn't what holds my attention.

Centered above the fireplace is a hand-carved sign that says "Home". Surrounding the sign is a smattering of framed photos, varying in size and orientation. I step closer and realize the photos are of us, the legacies. Almost every photo we've taken together in the last twelve months have been hung in the hub of our home.

My heart catches in my throat as my gaze flits from one image of smiling faces to the next. Tears leak out of the corner of my eye. "This is amazing," I whisper, turning back to look at Vlad.

"It wasn't just him," Leif states, casually strolling into the room. He doesn't fully reach the living room, stopping to lounge against a nearby wall like a languid cat. Marc, Tony, Alex, and Sylvia filter in behind him, walking further in to join Vlad.

"We wanted to bring your idea to life, to create a safe space for everyone. But more than that, we want to make this place into a home... our home," Sylvia says.

"You were in on this too?" I ask, glancing at each of my friends in turn.

"Of course, we're all in this together."

I run to Sylvia, wrapping my arms around her in a

grateful hug. What a sly minx. She probably snuck in here earlier when I had a phone call with my parents. The guys slowly join the hug, wrapping around us until we're one giant group.

Leif is the first to break away. The casualness in his voice sounds a bit forced as he asks, "Are we going to stand around the living room hugging all day? Or do you want to see the rest of the house?"

One Month Later

"MIRA, ARE YOU OUT HERE?" Sylvia's voice calls, echoing through the trees.

I round the corner, from the far side of the spring. Following the sound of her voice while simultaneously searching out her oompa-loompa orange hair. It's easy to spot and I rush towards her, covering half the distance before she notices me.

"What's up, Sylv?"

"Hey," she returns, her gaze drifting down my body. "Why aren't you ready? The ceremony is in an hour, you need to get dressed!"

"Oh crap! I lost track of time," I exclaim.

Dropping the leaves, I had been plucking off trees to admire their texture, I scurry towards the gravel path that leads back to the compound. Sylvia catches up within seconds and grabs onto my arm. She pulls me with her as her long legs eat up the distance quicker than mine.

We pass rows of chairs being set up in the yard of the main building to the compound, centered in front of a small stage. Further in the distance sits a large white tent containing tables, a dance area, and caterers milling about as they set up the elaborate feast we have planned for later.

My gaze flits over everything approvingly as we rush by. Tonight is an important event. It required a lot of effort to coordinate the moving pieces. I'm grateful the only thing that seems to be running behind is... well, me.

I push myself to move faster at the thought. Rushing up the stairs with Sylvia hot on my heels, I dash down the row of closed doors until I arrive at her room. Normally I would get ready in my own room, but we had pre-planned for this. My dress, which is remaining a surprise to everyone but Sylvia, is waiting in her closet.

The second we burst through the door, Sylvia pushes me down into the chair behind her vanity. Her grinning gaze meets mine in the mirror. "Are you ready for this?"

Inhaling deeply, I nod. "As ready as I'll ever be."

She squeezes my shoulder gently as she releases a soft laugh. "Well, let's get this show on the road.

Sylvia pokes, prods, brushes, and plucks me until I

barely recognize the heart-shaped face staring back in my reflection. "Wow," I whisper. I turn my face right to left, watching the light shimmer against my highlighter and bounce off the soft ringlets framing my face.

"You look amazing, Mir," Sylvia agrees, standing back as she assesses my face in the mirror. "Now, let's get you in your dress," she squeals, holding up a garment bag.

She unzips the case revealing my gown and I gasp, still as surprised by its beauty as the day I chose it in the store. Together we wriggle me into the beautiful white masterpiece. With a square neckline, flowing skirt, and shimmery glitter overlay, I feel like an absolute princess.

Turning away from the mirror, I'm suddenly concerned Sylvia spent too much of her time on me when she needed to focus on herself. "Do you have enough time to get ready?" I ask.

She waves her hands in front of her face, imitating a magician's assistant during a big reveal. "Girl, I'm obviously ready. All that's left is my dress."

My gaze skims over her smokey eye and nude lip, and I nod. "Okay, do you need help?"

Together we maneuver a silky, silver, tea-length dress over Sylvia's coiffed hair. After I tug up the zipper, Sylvia and I stand in front of the mirror together. "I'm so proud of us," I whisper, my eyes watering as I stare at our reflection.

Her eyes connect with mine in the mirror, the

cerulean blue orbs shimmering with humor and a little bit of the overemotional weepiness I'm experiencing. "We don't have time to cry, we need to head downstairs." She offers me her elbow. "Ready?"

Linking my arm into hers, I reply, "Ready."

Together we drift downstairs, and I wait in the small office, as Sylvia proceeds me outside. I continue to wait until I hear my queue, a musical symphony rising above the voices outside and quieting them.

I walk down the aisle separating the chairs, my white gown billowing lightly behind me. The seats are filled with guests, some that I know and some I don't, but hope to know soon. When I reach the small stage at the end where all my friends are already standing, waiting in formal wear, I smile lightly at each of them. I save Vlad for last, giving him a long, lingering, searing look before I turn to face the microphone.

"Some of you know me, but I'd like to introduce myself for those of you that don't. My name is Mira Love, and I'm pleased to welcome you to the Alliance. Our mission here is to…"

The End(ish)

NOTE FROM THE AUTHOR

Thank you so freaking much for reading The Curse Trilogy! We hope you loved reading about Mira, Vlad and their kooky group of friends as much as we loved writing about them.

Although the mysterious Curse affecting their world has been cured, we are not sure if Mira's story is quite over yet. It really feels as if Mira is just coming into herself and her power, meaning she has a lot of life to live and story for us to read still.

If you're interested in reading more about Mira and the gang, please please leave a review. Reviews are the lifeblood of any book, but they also help us authors to identify whether we're writing stories our readers enjoy.

If you're interested in reading more of our work, or staying updated on book news, please feel free to link up with any of the socials included on the next page.

Until next time!
    Nicole Marsh & Cassy James

INTERESTED IN NEWS ABOUT BOOKS BY NICOLE MARSH?

Check out her socials here!

INTERESTED IN NEWS ABOUT BOOKS BY CASSY JAMES?

Check out her socials here!

BOOKS BY NICOLE MARSH

The Curse Trilogy (Paranormal Romance)

Cursed

Bound

Shattered

Standalone

The Con

BOOKS BY CASSY JAMES

The Curse Trilogy (Paranormal Romance)

Cursed

Bound

Shattered

Rockin' Love Duet

Electric Wounds

Intoxicating Hearts

REVIEWS

If you enjoyed this book, please consider leaving an honest review. Reviews truly are the lifeblood of any book and your opinion matters.

Made in United States
Cleveland, OH
10 September 2025